THE LADY CAREY

Royal Court Series

ANNE R BAILEY

Edited by
VANESSA RICCI-THODE

Inkblot Press

For my dearest friend Ana-Maria

Also by Anne R Bailey

Forgotten Women of History

Joan

Fortuna's Queen

Royal Court Series

The Lady Carey

The Lady's Crown

The Lady's Ambition

Other

The Stars Above

You can also follow the author at: www.inkblotpressco.ca

Prologue

T he silence of the night was broken by the shouts of a group of men staggering to find their way back into the palace after an evening of frivolity in the taverns of London.

The bargeman that had carried them across the Thames cursed at them under his breath. He had been knocked back by an elbow and could have fallen into the river if he hadn't caught himself. Nor had they paid him much for his troubles. He fingered the coin and tucked it away. Perhaps he would buy himself a pint of ale.

The jolly men were oblivious to the activity happening in the palace, but someone finally noticed the candles were still lit at this late hour and wondered out loud what was happening.

A man broke away from the group and, when asked where he was going, told them he needed to relieve himself. Unlike the others, Edward was not half-drunk. His mind was whirling as he ran through the gardens and passageways to enter the palace through a more direct route to the King's chambers.

The physicians were heading away from his rooms. Edward grabbed a manservant, pulling him to the side.

"Sir, let me go! I am about the King's business."

Edward was undeterred by his protests. "What is happening? Is the King well?"

The manservant, recognizing Edward, took a breath and leaned in. "It's her majesty the Queen. She's gone into labor."

With that, he spun on his heel and left the courtier to think about what he had said.

It was too soon for the Queen to be delivered of a healthy babe. She was not in labor, she was miscarrying her child — Edward did not have to think long about what he would do next.

The next night, he waited in the depths of darkness for his compatriot to arrive. There was a sense of anticipation about him as he tapped his foot and paced the alcove. He had been unable to sleep properly, but it was excitement that had kept him awake.

"You wished to see me." Sir Bryan, Edward's co-conspirator had appeared.

Both men were shrouded in darkness, it would be hard to distinguish who they were much less see them. Then again, there were spies everywhere, even in the garden.

"With this latest development, I think it is time." Anticipation and hope spilled forth with each syllable.

The other man chuckled. "You are too eager."

"There is no longer any reason for you not to support us. The true Queen, God rest her soul, is buried."

"Amen, but our allegiance is with Princess Mary and to see her restored to her rightful place."

"Exactly, I could achieve this for you."

"How?"

"Jane has the affections of the King, and she could

persuade him to restore the Lady Mary." Edward stressed her new title.

"Jane? Don't tell me the King is looking to her as his new wife."

"She is the perfect example of womanly virtue and obedience, unlike the concubine." He referred to the current Queen by the nickname the Spanish had given her.

Sir Bryan laughed again. "Was she not caught by the Queen, sitting on the King's lap? Is that what you would call a virtuous woman?"

Even in the dark, the scowl on the man's face was evident.

"My sister is a most chaste and virtuous woman. There is no blemish on her reputation, and I shall make sure the world knows it." He collected himself. "The King is furious with the Queen over the loss of her babe and told me himself that he wonders what sins she has committed to be punished so."

There was silence as the other man considered. "I believe something can be done. If we have your promise that you and your family would support Princess Mary and help restore the true faith in England?"

"We shall do everything in our power," Edward promised, feeling assured that the King, seeking to please his new amour, would bend to her will.

"Then we shall meet again."

The schemers could not foresee the effect their decision to bring down one woman would have. England would never be the same.

Chapter One

C atherine bit back a complaint as the rented litter jostled her yet again.

Across from her sat her mother, the beautiful Mary Boleyn, with a past that would make anyone blush. Even in her thirties, her mother had retained her smooth skin, rosy cheeks and full mouth. But now her face was distorted by anguish and fury.

They were traveling with all haste towards London. They would not stop, could not stop.

As the driver swerved to avoid an obstacle in the road, Catherine was nearly thrown from her seat. Her stepfather could not afford anything more grand or comfortable. She had not come from meager beginnings. Her family was at the height of its power when she was born. But when her mother married the common-born William Stafford, she had been banished and, thus, impoverished. They had not spared Catherine, nor her younger brother Henry, when they sent her mother away from court.

Love cannot keep you fed. Catherine remembered one of

her mother's many quips and wondered why she had not listened to it herself.

It seemed that things were changing for the family yet again. Catherine stared at the crumpled letter in her mother's clenched fists.

It had arrived just after they had finished dinner. The messenger had taken his time arriving with this important letter. Perhaps it had been intercepted before being sent onwards. She had watched from the door as her mother nearly collapsed while reading the letter. Her stepfather was at her side in a moment, whispering words of comfort. Catherine wished she knew what it said. She had recognized the royal seal and knew it must have been an important message from the court.

Catherine was only eleven years old now, but even she knew that the fount of all wealth and power came from the court and the King. Her mother had caught her in the hall-way, and she'd thought she would be lectured for eavesdropping. Instead, her mother had ordered her to tell the maid to pack her things, for they were to go to London.

She hoped that her aunt, the Queen, had sent for her to be a maid-in-waiting. It made her heart beat with excitement just to think of the prospect. Perhaps her mother was sad to part with her and that was why she was being so theatrically grim. Mary's eyes had not wavered from the road as they had set off.

Catherine was not a fool, though. If her dreams had come true, then there would be no need for such haste. They would have sent a proper retinue to escort the pair of them to London, not just two manservants of her stepfather's. Catherine would have been ordered new gowns. She would have had a proper send off. No, something else had happened, and, whatever it was, it was not good.

She shivered.

The long hours passed, and the party passed through the gates of London just before curfew was called and the city gates would be closed.

Catherine felt aches all over her body after the hard travel. The houses and streets they passed did not interest her as they would have done.

Finally, she could sigh with relief as the litter came to a halt, and the driver helped them out. Wobbling with the first few steps, she turned to ask her mother what they would do now, but she found her mother was already walking towards a man dressed in black livery. Catherine tried to get a good look at the coat of arms on the man's chest and recognized the crest of her grandfather, Lord Wiltshire.

"Take me to my father, the Lord Privy Seal." Mary's voice was sharp and commanding, unlike the normal soft tone Catherine was used to hearing.

They followed after the man as he led through the winding corridors of the palace. They could have been walking in circles and she would not have known.

The man slowed his pace as he reached a pair of doors, another man standing guard beside it. They nodded to each other, and the second man stepped aside to let the first lead them inside.

"Lady Mary Boleyn and Lady Catherine Carey," he announced to the shape of a stooped man sitting in front of the fire.

"Leave us." A gruff voice gave the order, and the man disappeared from the room.

"You should not have come."

"I had to. How could I abandon her now?" Mary was incredulous as she watched her father.

He laughed. Catherine felt it was an inappropriate sound for such a somber moment.

"I wrote to warn you to stay away from court." He sighed as if the worries of the world were placed on his shoulders alone. "But I forget what a fool you are sometimes, not quite as clever as her."

"I am no fool." Mary took a breath. "I just did not have the ambition Anne always had, but look where that has taken her!"

Catherine grasped for her prayer book that hung from her side. She desperately wished she could slink away from the battle broiling before her.

Thomas Boleyn was on his feet in a moment, as if he had been struck. Perhaps he was not used to Mary snapping back in response to his abuses.

It was then he noticed Catherine standing there petrified. He fell back into his seat as though his breath was taken out of him.

"You should not have brought her." He waved Catherine away. "It will do us no good to remind him of the closeness the two of you enjoyed."

"You should retire for the night, Catherine. I'll speak to you in the morning."

Catherine was at a loss for what she was supposed to do and was exasperated that, after dragging her from her home, she was brought to court only to be abandoned.

Thomas Boleyn was also annoyed and snapped to a manservant to fetch his wife's maid.

After some length of time had passed, Catherine was led away. Before she left the room, she saw her mother take a seat beside her haggard father and ask him to repeat what had happened from the beginning.

Meanwhile, Catherine was enjoying the scrutiny of her

grandmother, whose severe features were intensified by the strain she was under.

"Grandmother," Catherine knelt for her blessing.

"You shall share your mother's old room."

"Will you tell me what has happened?" Catherine got straight to the point before she could be sent away yet again.

"Your aunt is to stand trial."

Catherine's eyebrows furrowed. How could a queen stand trial?

"For what?"

"It would be better that you did not know."

"And we are here to defend her?"

The shrill laugh of her grandmother echoed through the room. "We are here to serve the King. Your grandfather sat on the committee to investigate the Queen's behavior. Your uncle..." She pointed a finger at her face to emphasize the point. "...is to be the judge at her trial and of my son, George." Lady Elizabeth Boleyn's face crumpled and she choked back a sob.

Catherine took a step back at her words. "Why?" Her voice quavered.

Her grandmother composed herself; she refused to show weakness in front of a child like her. "Now you've gotten to the crux of the matter. The Queen has displeased the King."

Catherine looked as though she wanted to know more. Was that all it took? The King's displeasure?

"Perhaps you will learn, and, if the family ever recovers from this, you will have better luck as a courtier. Now say your prayers and go to bed. I do not have patience for your questions now."

Catherine did not protest as she was yet again taken away. She was shown to a small room with a truckle bed in the center of the room and a small chest of drawers. The maid unlaced her gown and put her in one of her grandmother's nightshifts. It did not escape her notice that the quality of her gown was nearly the same as that of the maid's.

She shuffled uncomfortably and then said the maid could leave; she would plait her hair herself. The maid was more than happy to go. After she said her prayers, she climbed into bed feeling too cold to try to listen at the door. A small fire had been lit in the room only recently.

As she shivered under the covers and willed herself to sleep, Catherine couldn't help remarking that this was not what she had envisioned her first night at the Palace of Westminster would be like. Nor had her estranged grandparents shown much interest in her. Then again, they were not a very loving family.

Finding she could not sleep, she went to find her mother only to hear whispers coming from her grandfather's privy chamber. She looked through the keyhole and saw Mary kneeling before her father, holding his hand.

"Will she be found guilty? Is there really nothing we can do? And George? Surely, this is nothing but rumors..."

Thomas Boleyn held up a hand to stop her.

"It is done. The King wishes to put her aside, and he will do so. One way or another. We must try to come out of this intact."

Mary bit the bottom of her lip to stop herself from protesting. Catherine could guess what she was thinking. After all, no one was ready to put their neck on the block by standing up to the King. "But it is not just him, is it? Many people want her put aside. He must have another bride in mind. Just like it was with Katherine of Aragon."

"Yes. Jane Seymour seems to be his choice. The King does nothing to hide his feelings towards her, and the family is showered with gifts."

Catherine knew it was their family that had once enjoyed this good fortune themselves.

"You should not be seen here. It will do you little good, and it may end up pulling you into the trial as well."

"I have done nothing."

"Perhaps. That is up to Cromwell to decide. But even if you have done nothing, then you may still be required to stand as a witness."

"I would defend her," Mary swore, but Thomas Boleyn only laughed. Catherine moved back from the keyhole at the cruel sound.

"Not in her defense, child." His hand lifted her head up to meet his gaze full on. "But against her for there is no defense to her actions."

Despite the fire blazing in the grate, her mother had started shivering. Catherine could imagine her thinking that yes, perhaps she shouldn't have rushed to return to court. But how could someone abandon their sister so easily?

"When is the trial?"

"It is set for the fifteenth, but, with Henry Norris and the rest of them declared guilty, there is little she can say or do to dissuade the council."

"She must be so afraid." Mary rubbed her hands together, when an idea seemed to strike her. "Catherine could go to her, couldn't she?"

Thomas Boleyn looked unsure. To Catherine, it looked as though he was trying to judge what advantage it might bring to him. Perhaps he was thinking how it would affect the family's reputation and her own.

"She would be able to comfort her. To let her know that we pray for her."

He shook his head. "I will not be associated with a harlot. I would disown her if I could."

"You did not have any hesitation before to call her your daughter when she was in the King's favor. You do not have to do anything but allow me to send Catherine to her. It would be a small act. You are her father, do you not hold any love in your heart for her?" Mary was insistent and she seemed to have struck a chord in the man before her.

"I am ruined regardless. Yes, you may send her. Though you do her no favors. Think of her future and how this might affect her."

Mary scowled. "I do not plan to use her as a pawn as you have used me and all the rest of your children."

Her grandfather smirked. "This is the way of the world, but I will not argue with you now. Let's talk of something else."

Catherine snuck away from the door. Her thoughts trying to process everything she had heard.

The next morning she awoke in a strange bed to her mother's gentle prodding.

"You must wake up now, Cate." She was using her pet name, but her face seemed contorted as though she was in pain.

"I know that Queen Anne has been imprisoned," Catherine assured her mother, thinking her mother was stressed about revealing this piece of bad news to her.

Mary nodded and sat down beside her daughter. "I have something important to tell you and you cannot tell anyone. Promise?"

"I do." Catherine looked intently at her. All the sleep from her eyes was gone, and she focused on her mother.

"There will be a trial and she will be found guilty."

"Or they might find her innocent," Catherine reminded her helpfully, and this innocent remark made Mary smile. A smile that told Catherine she said something very foolish and naïve.

"Well, you are to stay here, and it shall be arranged for you to go visit your aunt. You will be a brave girl for me, won't you?"

"What do you mean?" Catherine gripped the covers tightly. "What about you? Are you going somewhere?"

"I am returning to Essex tonight. I need to be there for your father, and I cannot stay here any longer in case I endanger us any further."

"But if there is danger, then I should leave too." Catherine shook her head.

"I would like you to stay and help your aunt. You can be her lady-in-waiting, and let her know that I love her and tried to help her. No one will harm you. I promise you that. She will need your support."

Catherine felt apprehension rise in her throat, and she felt as though she might vomit. "I don't want to go to the Tower. I am afraid."

Her mother had a faraway look on her face. "Think of how scared she must be." She paused. "With no family or friends. She needs you and you need to do your duty to this family and to her." The finality in her words left no room for argument, but, surprisingly, the fear had gone out of Catherine too. Replaced with a sense of purpose and importance, she nodded.

"I'll go."

"Good girl." Mary patted her face affectionately.

Events were moving faster than Catherine could have anticipated. Mary oversaw the maid packing her things into a small little truckle bag. Just two dresses and a few clean linen sheets were put in, along with a few items including a comb and hair pins.

Mary kept to her family rooms, staying out of sight of the court at large, although it had been spread around that she was back. She feared that she might draw unwanted attention and was set on fleeing as soon as she could. Her anxiety was felt by Catherine who was trying to find the courage to do what her mother demanded of her.

"We must go speak with Master Cromwell," Mary finally said, once all preparations were made.

Catherine was daunted by the man who was rumored to be the center of power at court — for the moment at least.

"Chin up." Mary spared her a glance, seeing her daughter's face as if for the first time. "Nothing to worry about." She repeated this for what seemed like the tenth time that day. Catherine couldn't help wondering if she was just trying to fool herself.

Regardless, she followed her mother out of the room after rearranging her skirts and making sure her hair was tucked into place. She looked like a proper lady now, with a borrowed deep green gown and a modest headdress. At her neck hung her gold cross that was given to her by her grandparents at her christening. She was old enough to wear it now.

Having spent many years living in nearly every royal palace, her mother knew the way through the corridors and rooms without needing someone to guide her. Catherine stuck close to her mother feeling they were being stared at by people passing by.

A few times, she saw people whispering behind their hands as they walked passed them. Instead of looking away, Catherine met their gazes head on, despite the fear she felt inside. There was nothing to worry about, she repeated in her mind over and over again.

A large ramble of men came around a corner, and her mother moved to one side to let them pass.

Catherine could tell immediately they were important, not only by the way everyone around them seemed to give them deference, but also by the fine cut of the cloth they wore and the way they held their heads up high.

"Who were they?" she whispered to her mother.

"The Seymour brothers." Her mother did not explain further until she squeezed her hand, pressing her for more. "They are the King's new favorites. The King is rumored to be in love with their sister, and, besides lavishing gifts and favors on her, has ennobled her eldest brother Edward with the title Lord Beauchamp."

In response, she frowned with distaste.

"Our family profited in the same way, so don't look like that Catherine," Mary admonished her. "Great favor comes from the King, and one way to get it is through his love."

Catherine nodded and they continued on their short journey. It seemed they were expected, for a clerk gave the pair a quick curtsey and showed them inside to Cromwell's office.

Her first impression of the man was that he was not as domineering as she thought. In fact, despite the wide set of his clothes, she could already tell he was a lithe man with a crop of unruly black hair. Hardly what she had imagined in her own mind.

But as he looked up from his papers, there was also something almost threatening about the manner in which he studied them and the way, after adding a few words to his letter, he set the pen aside with meticulous care.

He did not bow. Instead he swept a critical glance over them, studying them as though he could see into their inner thoughts.

"What can I do for you, Mistress Stafford?"

Catherine bit her tongue at the insult to her mother.

But her mother merely smiled her courtier's smile and corrected him calmly. "Lady Stafford, my husband was knighted."

"Indeed. And I see you have brought Lady Carey with you. Perhaps not the wisest choice."

"So I've been told." Mary stepped forward. "I have a favor to ask of you."

His eyebrows arched as if amused by her. "The only reason anyone ever comes to see me is to ask for a favor or two, so this is hardly surprising. But I must warn you, if this is about your infamous sister, then I would tread carefully." Despite the light tone, even Catherine could hear the warning.

"I've only come to ask if Catherine may join her as a maid-in-waiting in the Tower for the duration of her imprisonment. I know it would be a comfort to her to have a relative with her."

Catherine did not think it would be possible for his eyebrows to go up any higher, but they did.

"She was never kind to you, was she? You wrote to me begging for money not even a year ago, and I had to intercede with your sister on your behalf. You show a surprising amount of loyalty to her."

Was this true? Catherine could not be sure, but she remembered how tight food and money was in the early months of her mother's new marriage. They lived in cramped conditions, taking out loans whenever they could and economizing on everything.

"Yes, and I shall never forget the help you showed me then." Mary bowed her head. "But Anne is also my sister, and I am not so fickle as to forget her now."

"Perhaps you should join her in the Tower yourself then."

Cromwell pointed out a sensible alternative.

"I have to return to my husband and care for the children." Mary met his gaze and steeled herself for further argument. She knew that if she might go into the Tower herself, then fingers might point in her direction as well. After all, it was no secret that she used to be the King's mistress. "Catherine is more than capable of taking my place."

Catherine felt her mother place her hands on her shoulders. "She will not be a trouble to anyone."

Catherine watched the two adults size each other up in the poignant silence that followed.

"So be it, but I have a condition." His dark eyes turned to Catherine, and she looked away from his gaze, unable to keep it. "You shall report to me anything she says and help to get her to agree to anything I might require her to sign or say."

"She is a child," Mary protested. She did not want her daughter going in as a spy to her sister but rather a comfort.

"Then she is too young to be placed as a maid-in-waiting."

"I'll do it." Catherine spoke up, though she was disheartened to hear how soft and high pitched her voice sounded.

"Brave girl." Cromwell nodded. "I shall arrange it. She may join her aunt tomorrow."

"Thank you." Mary curtseyed and Catherine followed suit. They were dismissed.

Her last glimpse of this impressive man was of him picking up the pen once more and scratching away on the document in front of him.

Instead of dining in the hall with the other prominent courtiers and her grandparents, who were making every attempt to appear as though everything was normal and their eldest daughter the Queen was not in the Tower, Mary and Catherine dined alone in their rooms. The food was prepared by Thomas Boleyn's own cook in the small kitchen adjoining the room.

"Will I see the King?" Catherine asked her mother curiously. This was the one great person of the realm she had not laid her eyes on yet.

"Perhaps you shall glimpse him at the trial."

Catherine nodded, her eyes moving to her food. She did not wish to think of where she was going tomorrow, even though she had all but volunteered herself for the job. There was something exciting, though, about being in the middle of all of it. There was real fear and risk, but she also felt the wonderful sensation that she was doing something that could help someone.

There was another secret reason for Catherine to want to be at court. Her real father was here after all. Though she hid behind the name of Carey, Catherine was a royal bastard, but, instead of being recognized like the Duke of Richmond and Somerset, she and her brother were hidden away.

She supposed it stung that the King did not seem to care for her one way or another. Perhaps he had forgotten she even existed. But she knew she had inherited much of his looks including her red, almost blonde hair. Her dark eyes came from her mother's family.

Still, she was curious to meet this infamous man, though she would never dare claim kinship to him.

When her mother had told her about her parentage, she had been drilled in the importance of utmost secrecy. Nothing could be gained from claiming a connection like that. It would stain her reputation and any possibility of a proper marriage.

This was yet another secret she would keep to herself.

"Soon this will all be in the past and you shall return to Exeter." Mary changed the topic. "I will look into hiring a dance master to come teach you some of the more intricate dances."

Catherine did not even dare ask for what reason. It seemed as though she would never be going to court now.

After the food was taken away, they moved to a card table. A line of white pearls decorated the edges, and, in the center, the Boleyn family crest was finely etched into the wood. Her fingers skimmed over the polished wood and pearls — it had been ages since she had seen something so fine.

Mary spoke, instructing her on what she should say to Anne.

"Try to be positive and make sure you keep the conversation light and pleasant."

"Mother, there is no need for you to chide me." She squared her shoulders back. "I would never cause her any stress."

"As for the other matter. It would be best you reported anything you hear to Cromwell."

"You mean for me to spy on her?" Catherine had thought they had merely agreed to his demands as a way of getting her inside the court.

"It would be best to do what he says."

Catherine frowned. "But mother..."

"He will have other spies around her as well, and he would know if you do not report anything, but you can keep some things to yourself." She paused, searching for the best way to explain this to her. "As long as it doesn't harm the family or yourself and if it does not hurt her anymore, then you should report whatever you hear. There's also another matter."

Mary shuffled the cards with the skilled hands of an expert player.

"You shall convince her to remain calm and agree to whatever the King demands. This is the only way she might gain forgiveness or any sort of mercy from the King. If she threatens to fight him, remind her of what happened to Katherine of Aragon." This she whispered, as she dealt out the cards. "Can you do this?"

Catherine nodded. "I will try my best."

"Good. I don't know if she will listen to you but it can't hurt."

Chapter Two

T hat night Catherine tossed and turned dreaming of the Tower littered with heads on spikes, and the cawing of black crows. When her mother woke her with a soft shake, she pulled the covers up to her neck.

"Must I go?"

Mary said nothing but laid out a gown for her and called the maid in to help her daughter wash and get dressed.

When Catherine finally exited her room, she was tired, feeling the stress of the moment too.

"Everything will be alright," she said when she noticed her mother hesitating as she saw her nervousness.

"Yes, it will. Now, there's Mr. Cavendish here to escort you. Remember what we talked about and be a good girl. Promise me?" She cupped her daughter's pale face in her palms.

"I promise." She stood straighter then curtseyed to her mother and Mary blessed her.

"Take care. Your stepfather shall come get you when this is all over."

"One way or another?"

Mary nodded and Catherine left the room following after the man who had been waiting patiently outside.

It was early morning, only the servants were awake running around the palace, setting it to rights.

They walked down to the river where a small barge awaited them. Mr. Cavendish helped her on board but did not speak to her as they set off. Nor did he say anything once they arrived, except that she would have to have her belongings searched.

The whole process was done with clerical efficiency. She saw Cromwell's power for the first time for herself. All it took was a word to the guard of the Tower for her to be shown in — no questions asked.

The old fortress was imposing. Not only was it sparse of any decorations and pleasantries that were present in other great houses, but its outdated stonework added to the impression of the importance of this castle. It functioned both as a castle but mostly as a jail for prisoners of the crown.

She followed closely behind the guard as he led her to the Tower housing her aunt the Queen. Catherine looked up before stepping inside and thought she saw a figure standing at a window overlooking the green.

"This way, Lady Carey." The man was farther up ahead and noticed she had stopped to look at something.

The winding stairs seemed to go on forever, but finally, they reached the barred door guarded by two yeomen. Without a word, they opened the door and let the pair through.

"Your grace," the man began, though it did not sound like he placed much respect in the title. "I have brought your niece to stay with you and keep you company."

In the dim light of the morning, Catherine got her first real look at her notorious aunt. The fiery woman she imagined was replaced by the erect woman standing before the fire. Her features, hidden by shadows, were illuminated as she stepped closer to them.

"That is wonderfully kind of you, Sir. You must tell his majesty I am grateful for this small comfort. If I may write a letter to him..."

He cut her off. "It was not the King but Cromwell that allowed her to join you, Ma'am."

"I see." Her eyes flickered over Catherine, looking at her as though she was yet another enemy come to watch her every move.

Before Anne could say anything else, he made his bow and left the room. Catherine jumped at the sound of the key locking the door behind him.

All eyes were on her as she stood near the door, and the thought to try to leave crossed her mind. Before she could do anything, Anne crossed the remaining distance between them and embraced her.

"My little niece, it has been too long since I have last seen you." She tutted over her red curls and pale complexion. "They've dragged you out of bed to come see me, haven't they? You should have been brought to court sooner and served as a maid-in-waiting."

Catherine thanked her and then, embarrassed, remembered to bob a deep curtsey and say "Your grace."

Anne rose her up and invited her to take a seat beside her near the fire. The other three ladies in the room tried to resume their sewing or reading sermons, but they all struggled to hear what was being said.

"I am afraid there is nothing much to do here," Anne said apologetically, then chuckled at her own words. "But we have plenty of conversation, books to read and sewing projects. Sometimes I am allowed to walk in the garden. It's all rather pleasant." She tried to smile but her lips merely quavered. It was then that Catherine saw the extent of her fear.

"My mother, your sister, sends you her love," Catherine blurted out. Not very diplomatically nor as smoothly as she would have liked.

"I am sure." Anne picked up a previously abandoned glass of wine and drunk deeply. "How is she? Still living in that farmhouse with that nobody she married."

The cool haughtiness of Anne's tone pierced Catherine. It was so cruel to jest about her mother's lot in life when she herself was in a much more precarious situation.

"She is happy and wouldn't change anything for the world." This was the right thing to say, for Anne laughed and patted her with cold hands.

"I am glad you have a sharp tongue in that head of yours."

"Do you have any news for me? Have you seen the King?"

Catherine shook her head, and, in response, Anne gave a little groan of displeasure. "You can't be of much comfort to me then."

"I am told my trial will take place in two days, but I know of nothing else besides that."

Catherine bit her tongue to stop herself from saying what she knew. There was no point in telling her aunt that the trial was a forgone conclusion and that she could only pray for mercy.

"I know that Duke of Norfolk will be acting as judge," Catherine offered.

"Yes, I heard. Ironic isn't it that my own kin will sit in judgement of me." Anne sighed as if amused by this observation, but, in truth, her hands quavered and she clutched them to hide it.

There was unsurprisingly little for Catherine to do except bear through the tense atmosphere and try to hide her own apprehension at the unraveling of all of Anne's hopes. She was sure that Henry might have been disposed to forgiving her but this did not seem to be the case. More than that, Bishop Gardiner was her only visitor asking her to confess on a daily basis.

This was something Anne staunchly refused to do. She would wait for the trial and declare her innocence.

There was another reason to hope. No queen had ever been beheaded yet in England, Anne was positive she would be sent to a monastery to live out the remainder of her life in exile. She had plenty of cutting criticism for the nuns, but, at such a crucial time, she always added that she could live with that.

Catherine never forgot that she had agreed to help Lord Cromwell with Anne, but she also didn't know how she could be of service to him from the Tower. She didn't know who to talk to or how to relay a message, so she didn't feel guilty about not doing so.

She remembered her mother's warning that she had to be honest as possible or else she might get in more trouble.

One day while walking in the gardens with the other ladies a man approached her.

"I have a message for the Lady Carey from her mother," he announced.

"What is it?" Catherine stepped away from the group.

"Let's talk over here." He led her a bit farther away and pulled out a blank sheet of paper to show it to her as if letting her read a message.

"Has she said anything?" he asked, seeing that the others were walking away.

"Nothing." Catherine shook her head. He rolled his eyes at her unhelpfulness but tried again.

"What does she say about her brother?"

"She never brings him up." He nodded. "But she does believe she will be sent to a nunnery."

At this, the man looked surprised.

"She prays a lot," Catherine continued, hoping this was helpful. "But she has submitted herself to the King's will."

"Thank you, Lady Carey."

"And the message from my mother?"

He gave her a small smile. "There was no message, of course."

Feeling like a fool, Catherine returned to the others.

"What is wrong?" Madge asked.

"Nothing, my mother isn't feeling well."

This was easy enough to believe, plus her own dour expression added credibility to the story.

On the day of the trial, the ladies helped Anne dress while Catherine, bidden by Anne, was reading a passage from the bible:

1 Peter 1:6-7 *"In all this you greatly rejoice, though now for a little while you may have had to suffer grief in all kinds of trials. These have come so that the proven genuineness of your faith — of greater worth than gold, which perishes even though refined by fire — may result in praise, glory and honor when Jesus Christ is revealed."*

Anne had set aside her fear and steeled herself for the fight ahead. She had debated with her maids and even with

Catherine herself, as if trying to prepare herself for the inquisition ahead. But there was little she could say or do.

Her posture was straight as she was escorted from the rooms. Catherine was not to attend her at the trial. In fact, all the ladies waited anxiously in the Tower, though not in silence.

"Hopefully, this business will be done soon," Madge Shelton said trying to pinch her cheeks. She was very vain about her appearance and staying in the dark Tower rooms was making her look sickly rather than fashionably fair skinned.

"Yes, and then I wonder if we shall see that Seymour girl on the throne." Another Howard girl laughed. "Can you imagine that pale horse-faced girl on the throne?"

"I would do anything to be in her favor; then at least I could be with her in the country and not stuck here."

"I heard she is returning back to court shortly. The King misses her too much."

Catherine, who was looking out the window for the first signs of her aunt's return, tried to listen to their every word with rapt attention.

Their true colors showed now that Anne was out of sight. She frowned. What sort of allies were these? They were turncoats. But she supposed they would all have to be. Siding with Anne might land you in prison, if not worse.

It was nearly afternoon when Anne reappeared. All eyes were on her as she entered the room, stiff backed. She was not the same woman who had left this morning. It was as though she had aged several years in the last few hours.

Catherine rushed forward and grasped her arm when she began to teeter. "Do you want some wine? Or hot ale?"

"I'll sit by the fire."

Madge took her other arm, and the two of them led her to a chair.

Catherine, who had more of an inclination with these things, stoked the fire and added another log to it.

"What happened?" she finally asked, but Anne just shook her head, then turned her attention back on the fire.

She sat like that for a long time then called for someone to play the lute.

Catherine did not leave her side, sitting at her feet and trying to soothe her in some way.

"It's over," Anne finally whispered. "And I've lost." She wasn't speaking to Catherine but rather to herself.

"Surely, there is hope," Catherine urged but her aunt did not even look her way.

Too many illusions were being shattered for Catherine these last few days. While the court was grand, it was also terrifying, and the illustrious figures of court were merely men and women in positions of extraordinary power. Power that could be taken away at any moment.

The next day, Bishop Gardiner reappeared, followed in by clerks and a document for Anne to sign.

She had been declared guilty of adultery and treason. Her brother and all the men had been condemned as well. Now she would sign the paper declaring her marriage null and Elizabeth a bastard.

"He shall be merciful if you comply." Gardiner tried to encourage her.

Anne was hesitant. Everything she had suffered for and worked through would be gone in an instant if she signed this paper.

"I'll give you a minute to think about it, Lady Anne."

Anne scowled when he no longer addressed her as Queen.

Catherine was at her side once more. "You need to sign. They'll send you to a monastery and you will be spared the axe. My mother told me to remind you of what happened to the last queen."

Anne pushed her aside. "I don't need reminding. I brought it about after all. How dare they!" she hissed. "You know that whore Jane Parker stood witness against me and my brother?"

Catherine shook her head, of course she did not know.

"I pray to God she will get what she deserves in the end. If I could, I would see her pulled down myself. And my poor brother, what shall become of him?" When she turned around Catherine noted with surprise the tears pouring down Anne's cheeks. They were tears of anger for her expression was fierce and it looked as though she was trying to stop herself from shaking.

"I cannot believe he will be gone."

"Don't fret," Catherine said weakly. She had never met her uncle or at least did not remember him too much. "Just sign the paper. It will do you no good to fight them on this."

Anne groaned as if she would protest, but, finally, biting her lip, she sat down and did it. Gardiner was called back in, and he thanked her for her compliance before leaving once more.

The next morning they were awoken to the sound of sawing and hammering.

"The scaffold." Madge was looking out the window.

Catherine was at her side in an instant. She watched the workers haul pieces of lumber while others positioned them. They seemed practiced at building scaffolds, a thought that made her cringe. After a while, she had to look away as it dawned on her that she was looking at the very spot where tomorrow her uncle would be executed.

Anne was staunchly refusing to acknowledge the sounds. Unlike the other ladies, she did not run to stare out the window nor did she break down in tears. She went about her day as if nothing was happening.

Eventually, the other ladies did the same. There was nothing to do except darn some shirts for the poor, read or take strolls about the room. No one wanted to play cards, sing, or dance in such dark quarters with the threat of death hanging over the place like a curse.

That night, Catherine, who was sharing a bed with her aunt, felt her shaking sobs before she heard them. Without moving, she opened her eyes and peered at the Queen's back. Anne was crying into her pillow, trying hard not to make a sound.

She thought for a moment about how to approach her but found she dared not.

In the morning, despite the noise outside and the other ladies pressed against the glass, Catherine picked up a lute and strummed a few chords, trying to drown out the horrible sounds of the crowd, the priest, the drums and finally the loud thud of the axe.

Anne did not miss a single second. She saw every last motion her brother made, and she clutched at the prayer book she held until her fingers were white with the effort. She would be a witness to her brother going to death as a traitor for a crime he did not commit.

They had such high hopes and yet they were all whisked away into nothingness with what seemed like a single action.

"At least it was a mercifully quick death." Madge patted Anne's hand, but Anne only fixed her with a glare and Madge moved away.

After the crowds had dispersed and it was quiet outside the window once more, Anne sent for her confessor Bishop Cranmer.

He appeared after some time and she took him immediately to the corner to talk to him as privately as she dared. In truth, she was all but whispering in his ear. Whatever he was replying, there was no way to hear since he turned his back to the group.

He did not stay long but did say the mass with the rest of the ladies and blessed them each in turn.

It was only after they dined that night that Catherine had the chance to speak with Anne.

"What did you ask him?" Her voice was hoarse from misuse.

"He told me my marriage was annulled formally and then told me when it is to happen," she took a deep breath and Catherine noticed her shaking hands. "It will be over soon."

Catherine couldn't bring herself to pry further, but she desperately wanted to know when Anne would be released and she could go home.

Everyone looked as tired and pale as Anne now. Any attempts to try to distract themselves failed when news reached them that the King sent for a French swordsman.

Only Anne remained immune to this new development and told the messenger to thank the King for his act of kindness.

For his part, the messenger stood there awkwardly and fled as soon as he could. A Queen of England was never beheaded before this, and, even though King Henry had promised some sort of exile for Anne rather than death, Catherine couldn't help but wonder why he was going through all this trouble if he wasn't going to go through with it.

This was not what Catherine imagined when she had prayed to be at court. This went beyond missing out on the luxuries. This was real danger. She had not been brave enough to see her uncle go to his death. She had shut her eyes to it but it had still happened.

She felt as though every hour dragged on. When she slept, she dreamt of the axe swinging down on her own neck and would wake in a sweat, a hand to her neck.

"There's no need for you to fear." Anne's voice pierced the darkness.

Catherine hadn't known she was awake as well.

"Will you be sent to a monastery?" Catherine asked the crucial question.

"I don't think so," was the eerie reply.

"But you seemed so sure this morning."

"I know there can be no safety for me. Not after all I have gone through and done, but, at the same time, I cannot just give up. While there is still breath in my body I shall go on fighting and hoping and never let them see how very afraid I am."

"And are you afraid?"

"Of course, I'd be a fool not to be."

There was a long silence after that.

"I told you this so you might tell your mother and my mother if you get the chance. That I went on fighting."

"I shall. I promise."

"Good. Go to sleep."

At her commanding tone, Catherine shut her eyes as though she was a child and the nurse had commanded her to fall asleep.

The French swordsman was delayed and they had yet another day of waiting anxiously to find out if one way or another Anne would be spared or killed. One way or another this would end.

Catherine kept her dour thoughts to herself. She clung to the secret Anne whispered to her and tried to emulate her stony silence.

That night Anne began pacing the room, her lips muttering over words. While it was clear she was practicing a speech, she refused to give voice to it.

Then she called for a last confession, as was proper. The ladies filed out of the room and gave her privacy in her chapel.

Catherine had the chance to slip away but she refused to even think of it now. She would wait with her aunt.

She moved as if in a dream laying out a gown of rich dark velvet with silver embroidery decorating the sleeves.

"I think this will be suitable," Anne said aloud, and, though Madge nodded, no one said anything else.

Catherine went to the window and saw that the apple tree had begun to flower.

The farm in Exeter must be in bloom too. She imagined her mother working hard in the dairy to make the cheese while her younger half-sister toddled around by her feet. William Stafford would be overseeing the help tilling the land. She knew how insecure he felt about being unable to provide for her mother the life she was accustomed too. Soon he hoped to hire more help around the farm, then they could enjoy more leisurely activities.

Henry was with his tutors, and, though he had been legally adopted by Anne, his future remained in Mary's hands. She wondered what would happen now that Anne was no longer Queen.

Perhaps Elizabeth would come stay with them now that she was no longer a princess either. There would be festivals and markets to go to in the summer, and, while it may not have been proper, Mary took her along to haggle for food and other necessities.

It wasn't a hard life, while it was occasionally dull. She never had to worry about spies or anything of that sort.

No matter how slow time seemed to be passing, morning eventually arrived.

Anne said her last confession with her priest and held Catherine's hand while they brushed and pinned up her hair. She left the Boleyn "B" necklace for last.

"I assume they'll want me to remove this." A laugh died in her throat.

"You look majestic." Catherine glanced outside the window. A large crowd had gathered, but she didn't care about them. She was looking for the one man who could save her. Her love and he wasn't there.

A knock at the door made everyone freeze. Catherine wanted to step in front of her aunt as if to protect her from what was coming, but it was a foolish thought. Anne had seen and done more things than she could ever imagine. She didn't need a small girl defending her.

First, an armed guard stepped in the room, followed by Gardiner and Cranmer walking as quickly as possible.

"Lady Anne," they greeted her with a mere nod of the head. "Are you ready?" Cranmer, the kinder of the two, asked.

Anne gave a curt nod of her head, and, with a swish of her skirt and a snap to her ladies, everyone was ready and took their places for the procession. Catherine had to will herself not to be weak or fainthearted. She tried to mimic the cold stare of Anne's and stood as straight as she could.

But more than anything, she hoped her mother would

appear and take her away. Then she could hide her face in the skirts of her dress as if she was a shy child again.

They slowly proceeded out of the rooms for the last time. Each step she took made her heart beat faster. Ahead of her, Anne gave no sign of distress. At the bottom of the stairs, a man with his cap in his hands bowed and revealed the open door leading to the green, the scaffold, the crowd and the empty chair.

With three more steps there was a collective intake of breath as they stepped out on the green.

The crowd began moving in unison, jostling to get a better view. Some were calling out profanities and others were shouting blessings, but they were soon silenced, not by the guards pressing them back, but by their curiosity to see a queen brought so low.

The proceedings were not new and though Anne remained calm — Catherine could tell by the small tilt of her head that she kept looking towards the river rather than remaining fixated on the scaffold.

Hope never died for the doomed.

She climbed the steps of the scaffold, and, as if by magic, she was transformed before the crowd resembling for the first time what Catherine imagined she must have looked like at the height of her power and beauty. Then, with unwavering strength and presence, she began speaking:

"Good Christian people, I am come hither to die, for according to the law, and by the law I am judged to die, and therefore I will speak nothing against it. I am come hither to accuse no man, nor to speak anything of that, whereof I am accused and condemned to die, but I pray God save the King and send him long to reign over you, for a gentler nor a more merciful prince was there never: and to me he was ever a good, a gentle and sovereign lord. And if any person will meddle of my cause, I require them to judge the best. And thus I take my leave of the world and of you all, and I heartily desire you all to pray for me. O Lord have mercy on me, to God I commend my soul."

As her speech ended, Anne paused. Her last words that she addressed to the congregation hung in the air. For Catherine, the words "by the law I am judged to die" echoed in her head over and over again.

Then Anne turned away and her ladies helped her remove her headdress leaving her in a plain white bonnet that looked austere against the black gown. Then her hands went to the back of her neck. Gingerly she unclasped the infamous necklace. When Catherine felt it pressed into her cold hands she nearly jumped away. She had been trying to avoid looking at Anne, not wanting to cry. But there was no avoiding it. For the last time they locked eyes. A moment that must have seemed like a second to others was an eternity to her.

The injustice of Anne's death was overwhelming Catherine now. How could all these people stand by and let her die?

Where was the King?

Catherine clutched at the necklace in her hands the gold B digging into her palm. Anne had turned around and was repeating "To Jesus Christ I commend my soul." Over and over again as they tied the blindfold.

Then she knelt.

It was over in a pitifully quick moment. True to his words, Henry had hired a professional swordsman to remove the head of his beloved wife.

Catherine must have fainted, for she woke up propped up beside an alcove on a makeshift wooden bench. She blinked and saw Madge beside her, the Master of the Tower was standing a bit farther away. The hundreds of onlookers had begun dispersing and it looked chaotic.

"Sorry, I didn't grab you in time," Madge apologized.

Catherine wasn't sure what she was talking about but her hand rose to her head and she winced at the pain.

"You hit your head," Madge explained, seeing the confusion.

"Oh."

"Let me see her," a deep voice demanded and Catherine saw a familiar man push his way through the crowd and past the Master of the Tower.

"Father!" Catherine called out in a moment of childish delight. He knelt by her side and looked her over.

"I saw you fall. Are you alright?"

Catherine nodded. "And Anne? Where is she?"

"They've taken her away to be buried." He spoke softly. "And I've come to take you home."

At the word home, Catherine began crying in earnest. More than anything she wanted to be there, away from the horrors of court and the Tower.

"I'll fetch her things," Madge offered. A surprisingly kind gesture.

"I'll leave her in your care then, Sir." The Master of the Tower gave him a small bow and then left to see to his other duties.

Trying to calm herself, Catherine dried her eyes repeatedly.

"You were very brave." He tried to assure her.

"No, I wasn't." Catherine admitted now that they were

alone. "I didn't want to look at her. I didn't want to believe it and then I fainted. I couldn't be strong like her."

William Stafford patted her hand. "Don't dwell on it. Now can you get to your feet?"

It took her a moment to steady herself, but, as the dizziness and sickness dissipated, she felt more resolute that she wanted to leave this place immediately.

As if summoned by her thoughts Madge appeared with her bag of things.

"There you are. The maid said everything should be tucked away." Madge held out of the sack and William thanked her.

"Take care. I should go find my mother." Madge looked right and left to see if she could spot her, but the large crowd of people had not yet departed.

"I have horses waiting by an inn if you are well enough to travel," William said as he led her away, letting her lean on his arm.

"I am," Catherine promised and seeing his skepticism she added, "I could not stay in the city another night. I want to be with my mother."

She knew how childish it sounded, but she also had another purpose. She wanted to tell her mother everything she had seen and heard. Anne was innocent — at least she believed that. She wanted to tell her the last words she spoke, for they were ingrained in her mind forever now.

Chapter Three

At length, they reached an inn and found the horses were saddled and ready to go. Catherine would ride pillion behind her stepfather and they would make their way home.

They had no trouble on the road, though passersby would ask them for news from London.

"Is the Queen dead?" was the frequent question.

William would nod and not stop, though they would have more questions. Some cheered while others shook their heads in wonder. King Henry had driven two women to their graves now.

By the time the sun had set, they reached Exeter. Catherine jumped down from the horse before William could help her down and was in her mother's arms in an instant.

Mary was crying into her hair as she held her daughter. Catherine's tears by now were spent, and she was able to tell her mother the last words of her sister at the end of her recounting of the last days she spent with Anne. She handed the pearl choker to Mary who blanched at the sight of it.

"No, she gave it to you."

"Mother, I believe she would have wanted you to have it."

Mary shook her head. "It is yours to remember her by."

Knowing it would be pointless to argue now, Catherine tucked it away in her jewelry box. A tiny but precious box filled with all her keepsakes collected over the years. It had a small lock and she kept it hidden under the fake bottom of her trunk. Now there would finally be something of value inside of it.

As she hoped, life in Exeter was as quiet and peaceful as she remembered it. The days were long and filled with work to keep her busy. If she wasn't helping feed the geese, or stir the pottage, she was mending shirts and watching her half-sister.

News didn't travel that fast but it didn't take long for word to reach them that the King had remarried a mere ten days after Anne's death. Mary had been expecting the news, but Catherine had balked at the maid when she repeated what she had heard in the village square.

Not long after two messages arrived.

The first was from Lord Cromwell confirming that the wardship of Harry Carey was reverting back to Mary Boleyn. The small manor home in Plashey was given to her as well. Unfortunately, she also had to write back asking for permission to sell the home to pay for Harry's tutors and other debts in the household.

The second letter was a surprise. After years of silence and neglect, Sir Thomas Boleyn had finally found it in his heart to forgive his daughter for her impudent marriage and invited her to come visit. The earlier conciliation had barely skimmed the surface of mending relations between the families, but it had been a beginning.

William looked pleased if not apprehensive about the news. He was notoriously stubborn and refused to give way to his father-in-law, especially after they had abandoned them to poverty.

When Catherine made her way to the kitchen, she found her mother's maid, Maggie, plucking away at a chicken, preparing it to be roasted. Removing feathers was always a pain and even the most skilled cooks couldn't get to them all. The smell of burnt feathers would permeate the kitchen.

Therefore, roasted chicken had to be seasoned to perfection.

Her mother was kneading, bread the one chore she found truly enjoyable. Catherine was sure it was a way for her to vent her frustrations. Whenever things went wrong or she argued with William, Mary would claim they were running low on bread and went to the kitchen to make more.

"Oh, Catherine, since you are here, why don't you help with the meat pie?"

This wasn't exactly what she had come in here to ask. She wanted to see when they were to go to Hever, but she supposed it would be better for her not to argue. Taking an apron, she wrapped it around herself, though she thought the dress was hardly worth protecting.

Her mother had much nicer things tucked away in trunks with heavy locks — carefully preserved with herbs to keep the moths out and the clothes smelling fresh.

For her part, Catherine was not too interested in learning how to run a kitchen.

She remembered when they had servants to do this sort of work. But as her mother said, she should be grateful for what they had. There were others with far less. Unbidden, an image of her aunt in the Tower entered her mind, and she bit her tongue to stop herself from crying or having another panic attack. She had been prone to those since returning. At night, she was haunted by dreams of the swordsman, and then there was the sound of the axe that ended her uncle's life just as quickly.

She stirred the pot of meat, adding the seasoning as her mother called out instructions to her. The pie dough was already laid out over a dish, ready to be filled.

Outside she could hear Harry returning from a ride in the woods.

Only he seemed to escape the chores on the farm. He was either busy with his tutors or taking lessons with other noblemen's children. His only duty was to watch William put together the household finances and taxes for the King. In his spare time he would practice jousting or riding in a makeshift pen that William set up.

What he really wanted to do was go hunting or hawking. Unfortunately, this was an expense that could not be afforded.

Their younger half-sister, Anne, was only two years old, and, though she was beginning to walk, all she could help Catherine do was throw feed to the chicken and geese they kept.

So the majority of the extra work fell on Catherine.

Once the planting was done, William agreed to pack up their small family and travel to Hever. Catherine was the only one more unwilling to go than William. She had dug in her heels at the thought of leaving the safety of the quiet farmhouse. But regardless of her opinion they were on the road towards the family estate.

The walled bailey was a predominant feature that stood out as the party approached. Catherine recognized it from her early childhood. The old gatehouse was reminiscent of the chivalric tales she heard growing up. Inside the walled gatehouse was a more modern family home. This was the house where her mother and aunt had grown up in while they were in England.

William helped Mary, who was dressed in her finery, down from her horse, and they greeted her mother and father who had been waiting patiently by the entrance.

There was no need for grand entrances or especially formal introductions here. They were no longer part of the royal family but rather they were a family of ill repute.

"You children must be cold." Elizabeth hurried them inside. Catherine, who was clutching to the tiny Anne, carried her in. Anne was shy and scared of this new house, and it took her sometime to be able to smile for her grandmother and father.

The adults retreated, leaving a maid to sit with her and Harry, who quickly grew bored waiting in the hall. He picked at books and stared at the portraits hanging from the wall. Catherine teased him about the conceited way he seemed to carry himself with his nose up in the air.

"I cannot help it if I was taught by the very best at court. Now I am here." He sniffed as if it did not matter much. Catherine scowled.

"I was at court too, and I'll have you know I'd rather be here than back there."

"You are nothing but a country bumpkin," Harry teased, but, for once, Catherine held back from sticking her tongue out at him or responding to his insults in any way. She was far more mature and grown up than Harry now.

Let him be a child.

Baby Anne was trying to suck on her thumb, a habit of hers whenever she was nervous. Catherine scolded her and took her around the room to explore.

Eventually, the adults returned and they went to dine in the hall. Though they ate far more richly than they did at home, the conversation was stilted and they mostly ate in silence.

After their meal they enjoyed listening to a musician sing a ballad and then were whisked off to bed.

Catherine knew how stressed her mother and stepfather had been on the first day. She was sure she found the second day just as grueling. They had been interrogated on their health, what they were doing and all the things they might have wished to avoid discussing from their finances to the state of their house.

Catherine had been in the room, distracting her sister with silly games. So she heard Thomas Boleyn's extended an invitation for them to take up residence in Rochford Hall.

"What about Jane?" Mary practically spat out the cursed name.

"She is at court."

"Still?" Mary was shocked Jane had managed to hold on to a position.

"She has a powerful benefactor."

"Who?"

"Your uncle," Thomas Boleyn said with a shrug. "But while she may be serving the Queen, she does not have any rights to Rochford Hall. That property reverted back to me."

Mary looked to William, but it was clear they would have to talk later.

One topic was glaringly not discussed. Anne and George. Perhaps the topic was too fresh and painful or her parents had moved passed it as if they were failed projects.

But Catherine knew that upstairs in one of the many rooms of Hever was a small portrait of Anne. She had walked passed it and had felt her heart clench in painful remembrance. Anne had become more popular in death than she had ever been in life.

The common people pitied her now, but that would do her little good.

They had the luxury of a private sitting room, and Catherine was tasked with serving her parents wine and fetching things for them. She stood resting against the wood panels of the room and waited for a request but also listened as they spoke.

Mary, who was lounging on a couch, had turned to William, ready to talk about what her parents had said.

"This is a wonderful opportunity for us and the children, don't you think so?" Mary began coyly. Even Catherine knew he had reason to protest. He treasured his independence, which would be threatened if they did move to Rochford Hall.

"I think this is your family meddling with things they shouldn't be meddling in."

"What do you mean?" Mary propped herself up on her elbows.

"Your father probably has some far-flung hopes of regaining influence."

"I would never return to court nor serve them in any way." She jumped to reassure him, causing him to put a hand over hers.

"Peace, wife. I know you wouldn't, but there are your eldest children to consider. They will be made into courtier's one way or another, and little Catherine has proven that she is no fool. The future lies with them. They are the next generation of Boleyns and Howards."

Mary bit her lip. "It could be a profitable future for them. It could give us a reprieve too."

His eyes darkened at what he saw as an insult, and she hurried to add, "Let us use them as they would use us. As they have taken advantage of us in the past."

He leaned over and kissed her brow. "Of course, if this is what you want. But I shall not have your father hold it over my head that I have taken his charity."

"I am his heir, it is my right. This would not be an act of charity."

William seemed reassured by this and eventually they retired for the night, sending Catherine to her room as well.

They were pampered at Hever that summer. Besides not doing any hard labor, they were treated to sweetmeats, pastries, cakes, puddings and plenty of entertainment.

One night, Catherine found herself pretending that she was dancing before the King. She was pushing thoughts of the Tower away and focusing on the happier stories she heard about court. She came out of her thoughts when her brother gave her a pinch. She was no longer dancing with a handsome stranger, she was prancing around with Harry. He liked to tease her about the faraway look she got when she danced, and she would pinch him in return.

It took all her nerve and restraint to keep from hollering or yelling at him. She had to act the part of the lady and saw it as a personal victory when she got through a set without making a peep.

The adults applauded as the dance ended and they took a bow. Catherine smiled radiantly, although underneath the smile she was thinking about how she could pay back her brother.

As the men retreated, the women settled down for a game of cards.

Her grandmother called her over. "You can play with me child." She winked. "I'll teach you all my tricks and you shall make your fortune."

"Isn't gambling a sin, Mother?" Mary asked.

"Only when you lose. Besides it is better to have the skills to defend yourself. Ignorance is also a sin." Elizabeth cracked a weary smile towards her daughter shuffling the cards.

Catherine was not completely ignorant of courtly entertainment, but her grandmother proved to be quite deft with her cards.

"This game is called Imperial. You need to make a suit of cards to win," she explained and played a round with Mary; then she invited Catherine to join in the game. "Polite conversation is also always essential when one plays cards." She prompted her to speak, but Catherine was tongue tied, leaving her elders to pick up the conversation.

Finally they turned back to her. "And how are you at chess?" Elizabeth asked, seeing how poorly Catherine was playing.

"I play a fair bit." Catherine felt awkward about the interrogation.

"She beats Harry all the time," Mary bragged, but Elizabeth turned the compliment on its head.

"Is that because of her skill or your boy's lack of it?"

"He's a smart boy."

"Too foolish." Elizabeth shook her head.

"He is only nine years old." Catherine defended him.

"At least we know she is loyal to the family." Elizabeth then called for some wine and they returned to playing cards in earnest.

All sorts of questions followed the next few days. From her skill with the lute — which she barely had any — to her other strengths and weaknesses.

"She has a good head for numbers and can read and write in French, Latin and English."

"Barely, in Latin." Catherine corrected her mother who was bragging so much that she was sure she had to confess every day.

The two women seemed to be conversing about something more than just her abilities. She got the sense that they were two fishwives at the market bartering over the quality of their wares.

Could her grandmother be thinking of a betrothal for her? Or to find her a position at court?

Her heart pounded at the thought, and she willed it not to be so.

She wasn't ready to leave her mother. Catherine knew that her own mother had married for the very first time at the age of fourteen. This meant that she could be betrothed in a year and married in two herself.

The thought was terrifying, but at least she wouldn't have to worry about the block. In either case, Catherine never found out the reasons behind all the questions and this first visit came to an end.

She left with promises of gifts to follow her. Already she was leaving with two of her grandmother's old gowns to be cut up and resewn to suit her. The fine velvet was the most precious thing she owned.

Chapter Four

They had returned home for two months before the move to Rochford Hall was finally announced to the whole household.

This was news to Harry who let out a loud whoop of excitement. He had been raised in some of the nicest and well-furnished homes in England. Though he had never outwardly shown his contempt for the poverty he lived in now, Catherine knew her brother better. Knew enough to know that he blamed Anne for the loss of his position and power.

Even though he had his expensive tutors, this was not enough for him. Catherine joked that he had inherited ambition enough for the both of them.

"First we have to settle affairs here before moving to Rochford, then pack our belongings..." William trailed off seeing that Harry was already captivated by the idea and wasn't paying attention.

Catherine, on the other hand, made a face, her brow wrinkling.

"Nothing to worry yourself over," William said dryly.

Finding someone trustworthy to run the farm without much of a wage offered was hard enough but then there was also the uprooting of the household. Only her young sister's nursemaid would come along. Her mother's maid, Maggie, would stay behind to work in the dairy and look after the poultry.

So they were delayed a month before they could set out.

They traveled ahead on horseback while their possessions were taken by a pair of oxen and a cart. William stayed behind to keep pace with the cart, while Mary and the children rode on ahead.

The journey took a day but the house at the end of it was worth the effort. Rochford Hall, which had only been recently built by her grandfather, boasted three floors of modern luxury and was situated on extensive land large enough to house a hunting park.

This was something Harry was itching to go try out. William had promised to take him hunting once they were settled in, and already Harry was asking for another horse that would be more up to the task.

Catherine hoped he would be lectured, but her mother ruffled her son's hair and promised to look into it for him. Perhaps money was no longer such an issue. She noted the exterior which had been built with expensive stone brick and featured large window panes that reflected sunlight back at the party.

The servants had opened up the house, airing out the closed rooms and putting fresh rushes on the floor. The house smelled of sweet lavender and clean linen.

Mary greeted the steward of the household and then took her eldest children on a tour.

"You were probably too young to remember this place, but I took you here one summer and you played in the fish pond." She pointed to the pond in question. "Catherine, you told me that you were going to turn into a fish and spend all day in it." Mary laughed at the fond memory but Harry teased her.

"She looks like a fish now. Look at her gaping." This earned him a swat on the head from Mary.

Catherine let the insult roll off her shoulders. This house was palace enough for her, and, at the moment, she couldn't believe it would be hers to live in.

Rochford Hall sported an equally large household. Much larger than what anyone in her immediate family was used to except for Mary and Harry.

There was nothing for Catherine to arrange or ask for. In the morning, a maid appeared to help her dress and get ready. She was the youngest daughter of a wool trader, and she had been assigned to take care of her personally. The maid would sleep in her room from the first night onward.

Catherine stood by as her mother met with the steward and the comptroller. Thomas Boleyn had provided them with the hopes that Rochford Hall would continue running smoothly. William practically pouted and accused him of meddling but had to agree to letting the steward oversee the household and make the necessary purchases as well as paying and assigning the servants.

Catherine had been in the room when William had stormed into her mother's solar demanding to know why he wasn't to be trusted.

"You are a gentleman," she tried to placate him. "Just as

you served in the King's household so must you let others serve you in your own home."

"It's an outrageous expense. I could oversee all the work and not feel as though your father was giving us more charity."

"You can still work and find plenty to do. At least you will have more help now." Mary's soothing tone always seemed to stop him from flying into a more serious rage.

Thus, Catherine saw firsthand the old saying put into practice; that you catch more flies with honey than with vinegar.

At first Catherine was up before her own maid but there was nothing for her to do yet. There were no chickens to feed nor food to prepare. She even dressed herself leaving nothing for her maid to do but brush and plait her hair. Since she wasn't married, she didn't wear a cap or headdress everyday like her mother did.

There was another surprise for her at Rochford that came in the form of books. She didn't bother with any of the heavier subjects and histories. The large tomes on History and Theology were left to gather dust as she perused books on poetry and chivalric tales. Even those on hymns and prayers were taken down.

"Too much reading will hurt your eyes," Mary said.

Catherine shrugged at the warning.

"So does sewing." Which earned her an angry glance from her mother.

Henry seemed to thrive as well. He loved hunting and prided himself on keeping up with the adults when they went.

The deer in the park had not been hunted for nearly a year and had fattened during this time. Their slower pace made them easy pickings for now and venison graced the great table every week. Catherine felt herself growing plumper by the week from the rich food and leisure.

She took to walking through the orchards and gardens in the afternoon. Picking a ripe pear or apricot to enjoy as she breathed in fresh air.

Some days she watched Harry practice jousting on his pony.

He would run at his opponent, who she pretended was a French knight, yelling "For England and St. George" as a battle cry.

Her mother didn't let her enjoy this reprieve for long and set her to work stitching shirts and practicing her lute.

Catherine hated the instrument, plucking the string endlessly left blisters on her fingers and she had no ear for music. She enjoyed listening to it, but, when she played, it was mechanical and full of mistakes. Her mother scolded her several times and her music teacher wouldn't hold back from slapping her hands every time she hesitated.

Her mother's attention waned quickly, and she found herself free to do whatever she pleased.

The grooms of the chamber learned in the early days of their arrival that their new master slept every night in his wife's chambers. They would wait patiently for the ladies to go through and only enter the room when bidden.

William was particularly peeved and amused by the way they hounded him.

"As if I cannot put on my own hose," he teased at the breakfast table.

Her mother would kiss his temple and send him to be dressed and cleaned for matins.

Unlike her stepfather, Catherine saw that her mother was in her element here. She no longer went to the market to haggle over the price of fish — they had their own fish pond now. No longer was she blistering her hands with labor around the house. In fact, her mother joined her in blissful rest.

Mary took up work on a new tapestry which she imagined would grace the wall of their new private dining room. She was having one of the old offices remodeled to serve this purpose. She didn't mind eating in the hall at the high table overseeing their servants and members of the household, but it offered her and William some privacy. She knew William would enjoy being away from prying eyes for the occasional family meal. Catherine followed at her heels, watching her instruct the carpenter on what she wanted and speaking to the steward about the funds for the renovation.

Her grandfather had been generous and let them make changes to the household as they wished. There was one person her mother took great pleasure in thwarting and that was none other than Jane Rochford.

The spiteful woman was living in a small house somewhere nearby in nearly abject poverty. It was no less than what she deserved. The self-styled Lady Rochford was exiled from her own house. Mary would never forgive her for betraying her brother, and Catherine would never forget that she had testified against Anne. Nor would she stop cursing her for the accusations she made. They were dirty and vile and had gone beyond what Cromwell needed to condemn both her brother and sister. More than that they were sure to stain the family for years to come.

So it was satisfying to know that she was now living in Jane's old home.

Their previous situation had left a mark on the family, and

Catherine watched as her mother strove to ensure Rochford became an industrious and self-sustaining house. She sold the pelts of the deer and other hunted animals to tanners to make leather and increased the size of the herb and vegetable garden, allowing more to be sent to the market to be sold.

While she had to defer to the occasional seamstress to fix dresses and adjust the cut of a gown, she hesitated to call on their services and mended and altered clothes herself as much as possible.

In the back of her mind, she was also always putting away money.

"We need to think of your future," she said to Catherine one day. "It won't be long before you are married or you are called to go to court."

"Won't I get paid if I go to court?"

Mary smiled at her. "But that will barely cover the cost of your gowns. Don't worry, we will manage."

Her mother was sitting in the solar early one morning, a spindle in her lap as she watched the sun climb higher and higher into the sky. Catherine was at her side practicing her needlework.

When her mother had been young, she had been sent away from her family to get an education in court of France. Then, when she returned to England, she went to court. She had hardly ever lived with her own parents and then she had been married too. Catherine preferred being kept at home. Nothing was more comforting than being able to run to her mother or stepfather for help or guidance. She also imagined holidays would be lonely without her family. Celebrating the New Year with strangers was not appealing.

Despite the outward appearance of domestic bliss, Catherine had noticed changes in her mother since the death of her aunt. She had become more religious and observed the fast days as strictly as she could. Mass was attended at least once a day and she did not allow for any lewd or debauched behavior in her household. All the members of this house had to be dutiful Christians. She wouldn't tolerate heretics anywhere near her home.

At times Catherine found this hypocritical— after all, it was widely known that she had been the King's mistress.

But even the church was no longer safe. Something was happening but Catherine could not be sure what. She knew that King Henry broke with Rome in order to marry her aunt and that this had displeased the people of England who saw the Pope as God's representative on Earth.

Now King Henry was the head of the church, but people were not happy. Catherine just did what she was told as she was sure all the courtiers did as well. They only had to look to the Tower where the heads of some of his most favored companions and friends had been hacked off and displayed for disagreeing with his religious views.

But the farther away you moved, the less his influence was felt, and people felt safer showing their displeasure about his decisions.

Her mother had told her not to worry about anything she heard.

"Just keep your head down and do as the King commands."

But then, in their little hamlet, there had been an uproar about the novel idea of the English Bible.

Then a silent shock at the taking down of all the finery from the chapels and altars. The King ruled that this was illegal.

So Catherine had watched her mother take inventory of the embroidered cloth, the chalices, relics and crucifixes being packed away into boxes to be stored or sent to Cromwell at his request.

Now the news of orders to dissolve the monasteries was being sent out by Cromwell's men. The people were moving into action against the tyranny of Cromwell. She found it ironic that the people had once blamed Anne for such misgivings, but, in fact, Henry was behind these changes. Perhaps she was to be blamed for putting the idea in his head, but soon the people would learn that this was his desire.

That their Prince had become a King with the whims of a child throwing a tantrum.

Catherine was interrupted from her sewing by the peeling of bells. She looked up at her mother, whose hand went instinctually to her growing stomach.

"What is it?"

Mary listened for a moment before replying.

"It must be good news from London. Go ask your stepfather if he knows anything."

Catherine was more than happy to put aside her sewing and went off to find him. He was receiving a report from a layman who had heard the proclamation.

"The Queen is with child. God bless her, and the King has ordered a mass of thanksgiving in all the counties throughout the Kingdom."

"That is most happy news," William said.

The man left and Catherine approached. "So the King's wait is over now."

William made a motion with his hand to caution her from speaking so brashly, but she was cautious enough. She had heard from her grandfather during his last visit how the King had become impatient just months after his new marriage. It had taken Jane about a year to conceive.

"Yes, and we shall pray that the Queen is delivered of a healthy child."

"And son," Catherine added.

No one who overheard the interaction would have known of the sarcasm behind Catherine's comment. She returned to her mother's rooms and told her the news.

"His short patience is becoming legendary," Mary said, nipping at a tread. "I am happy for poor Jane."

"Are you really?" Catherine whispered.

"I do not envy her position. It takes a lot out of a woman to be raised to such high status and importance. Think of all the troubles and worries that are placed on her shoulders."

Neither of them spoke after that as they both thought about Anne, who had been driven nearly mad trying to satisfy the King. When she failed, her head ended up on a chopping block. They never openly spoke about her, but her ever-present memory lingered over the family, reminding them how close they had been to the throne and how far they had fallen.

As the Queen's pregnancy went on, more wealth and honors were heaped on to the Seymour family. Edward Seymour was made an Earl and her father gained lands.

Catherine's grandfather never failed to stop by to report all of the gains the Seymour family had made when he was traveling back from court. He no longer had a favored place among the courtiers and more often than not had to find his own accommodations. Being the proud man that he was, he would pretend to have business at home to return to.

When her mother had dared suggest he take time to spend at home, he went into a rage. He refused to retire to his country estates. The way he had looked at his own daughter made Catherine think that he blamed her for all his troubles.

He had left that very afternoon and proceeded back to Hever Castle to stew.

In truth, Catherine did not see him as an old man even though he was in his sixties and was one of the oldest people she knew. He always seemed ready to snap at any chance that came his way, but this was wearing him down too. Every time she saw him, he looked more sapped of strength. But that was her speculation, and she would never say it out loud. Not that anyone would ask for her opinion. After all, she was just a girl.

Then in late summer, he brought news that the Queen would finally have her coronation, although the date had not been settled.

"The King wants to commission a new coronation barge to rival the one the Doge in Italy rides out in," Thomas Boleyn said.

"Have they begun working on it?" Catherine's mother asked.

"No, the King just commissioned a miniature."

Catherine, who was standing against the wall ready to refill glasses with a pitcher of wine nearby, zeroed in on that. The King seemed to work in vague promises lately.

"He must be waiting to see if the child is safely delivered and its gender," Mary said after some deliberation.

"Yes, and if she fails to produce a healthy living son, then I will bet you that the King will not hesitate to look for another wife." Thomas was feeling ungenerous towards the Queen.

Mary shook her head, her own belly had grown so round and firm. She would enter confinement in a few weeks.

"We shall pray for her safe delivery," William said. "We are entering dangerous grounds." He looked around, and, even though only the immediate family was here, he couldn't be sure no one was listening in through the doorway or cracks in the wall.

Cromwell was always on the lookout for any insurrection. After the rebellions in the north had been quelled, he had only managed to survive by a hair's width. He was walking on eggshells around the King and only by providing the King with alternatives could he avoid taking the brunt of his anger.

The Seymours would be more than happy to see their former ally fall.

Mary was growing tired and reached out for Catherine to help her to her feet.

"I must retire for the night."

Harry also leapt to his mother's side, and her two children helped her up the steep stairs on either side.

Catherine was tempted to hear what else her grandfather had to say about the factions at court. She soaked up all the information as greedily as a starving man.

With Mary sitting comfortably on one of her couches, Harry retired from the room and left Catherine to tend to her.

"Do you want me to bring you up some tea?" Making posits was one of the things Catherine could do well.

"And give you an excuse to go hear what is being said?" Mary laughed at her expression. "Don't think I am such a fool that I don't notice you listening at each snippet of conversation you can. You have the ears of a fox, but it might get you in trouble if you stick your nose in something dangerous."

Catherine shrugged. "There is nothing dangerous here at Rochford."

"But, if you ever go to court or get involved with the wrong sort of people, you will end up in the Tower of London. This is no laughing matter."

Catherine nodded. She didn't need to be repeatedly scolded. Perhaps she had inherited the family's ambition and love of danger and excitement. Despite having seen firsthand what could happen to those who strayed and lost the King's favor, she was more than willing to try her hand at court life.

"You can read to me." Mary pointed to the book of hours she had placed by her bedside.

Catherine obediently fetched it and began reading. In her head she was reading to Queen Jane at court, earning a place as a favored lady.

Catherine followed after the maids with a pile of fresh linen in her hands too. She would be entering confinement with her mother until she gave birth, and, since there was no one else to come sit with her mother, she had taken up the post of her chief lady and watched as everything was organized appropriately.

The room was cleaned from top to bottom and the cradle was brought out. It had been used for herself and brother already. A holy girdle to help in childbirth was taken out of storage and finally the priest came to bless the room before the shutters would close off as much light as possible to the room. Herbs and all sorts of medicine had been prepared in the kitchen to be used when they were needed.

Catherine had never been witness to a confinement before, and, while her mother was adamant she would leave once the labor pains started, she was still fascinated by all the preparations that went into this.

Candles were brought in and a griddle was set up by the door so the priest could come and say mass to them every morning without entering the room. Two midwives were hired in and would live at Rochford Hall until the baby was delivered.

"When will you go into labor?" Catherine asked.

Mary laughed at her daughter's innocence.

"I forget how young you are. Sometimes you can be so mature and wise for your age. The baby will come when he is ready to come and God wills it."

"You think it will be a boy?"

"I don't know. I shall be happy either way." Mary gave her hands a squeeze.

Catherine shivered at their cool touch. "You should sit by the fire, you feel so cold."

She worried that her mother could be so cold during the height of summer. Right now she would normally be sitting under the shade of an oak tree, letting her feet soak in the cool river.

It did not take long for her to become stir-crazy trapped in the two rooms of her mother's.

"How can you stay in here?" she asked.

"You will have to learn patience. All good things take time. This is the way things are done."

"I wouldn't let anyone put me in confinement."

"It's not a choice you can make. Besides it is better for you and the baby to rest."

After three weeks of trying to learn how to be patient, Catherine was awoken by something wet as she slept in the bed with her mother.

She pulled the covers aside and wrinkled her nose, thinking her mother must have wet herself.

"Lady Mother." She nudged her until she awoke.

Mary knew instantly what had happened. "Oh! Catherine you had better fetch the midwives."

"What?"

"The baby is coming. Go get them and stay away."

"Are you sure?" Catherine was worried now and jumped to her feet. She pulled on a robe over her nightgown and was at the door in an instant.

"Yes, just go. They'll know what to do and tell the kitchens to boil water."

Catherine found the midwives deep in sleep outside in the solar on palette beds. She woke them up with a furious shake.

"My mother has gone into labor, go help her."

"Patience, patience child. It doesn't sound like her pains have begun in earnest just yet."

Catherine wasn't sure what she meant but went running to wake the maid in the kitchens.

By the time she returned, the midwives were inside with her mother. She stuck her head through the door and asked if she could do anything to help.

Her mother was pulling on the cords tied around the bed. Her mother had told her to stay away, but she wanted to be of help. Seeing her mother straining and sweating about the bed, going paler by the minute, made her want to run to her side, but she found herself unable to move as her heart began racing.

"Girl, if you want to make yourself useful, why don't you place a compress on your mother's forehead." One of the midwives pointed to a bowl with linen.

Spurred into action Catherine ran forward, and, though she nearly tipped over the bowl, she drenched the linen in the cool water scented with herbs and wrung it out. She came to her mother's side, but Mary turned to her with a grimace.

"You can leave, Catherine, this isn't for y-you."

Her mother moaned as another spasm of pain hit her. Catherine placed the compress on her mother's head, gently patting away at the sweat.

"I'm here."

She wasn't sure if that comforted her mother or not. When instructed, she gave her mother some special birthing ale and replaced the compress.

Finally, the midwives announced they could see the baby's head.

"Not long now, milady."

Indeed minutes later the baby was born. Her mother's screams as the baby was wrenched from her body nearly made Catherine faint, but she focused on holding her mother steady by the shoulders.

"You have a healthy baby girl!" They held up the squalling babe.

Catherine almost moved away from the bald squirming mass covered in blood.

Sensing her distress Mary told her to go tell her stepfather.

"Tell him he has a daughter, and then light a candle for me and say a prayer in the chapel. I need to rest."

Catherine didn't want to leave her mother but finally did as she was told. The baby was being cleaned and swaddled as she closed the door behind her. She washed her hands in a basin as they were covered in oils and other things from the room.

William was waiting with a mug of ale in his private study.

"Father, you have a new daughter."

He leapt to his feet at the sound of her voice. "And your mother? Is she alright?"

"Yes, she was when I left her. I heard the baby cry too." She didn't mention that she thought the baby looked horrendously ugly.

"God be praised! I must go see her." He ran past her. It was considered bad luck for men to enter the confinement chamber, but William was never one to listen to such old wives tales.

Catherine knew they would want time alone and headed towards the church to light a candle at the altar of Saint Margaret for the safe deliverance of her mother. When she finished with her prayer, she returned slowly to her mother's room to find the nursemaid had her new baby sister feeding at her breast.

William had left already.

"We've decided to name her Elizabeth after my mother." Mary told her. She was now propped up on pillows. Her voice seemed drained of all energy.

The midwives were carrying away the dirty and blood-stained linen.

Catherine didn't climb into bed with her as though she were still a child, and she was still horrified by what she had seen. Despite the new sheets, she could still see the spoiled ones. But she did pull up a stool and held her mother's hand.

"You will rest and get better." The hint of a question lay in her tone. She was surprised to see her mother so tired and weak. She had never been present at a birth before, though she had once seen a lamb being born in the field.

But the sheep was up and walking around within minutes of the birth.

"Yes." Her mother's eyes were fluttering closed.

A midwife came to her side and looked her over.

"She pulled through for now, just keep an eye on her and make sure she drinks and eats as much as possible."

Catherine nodded. She would do anything in her power to look over her mother.

In a few days she could breathe easier as Mary seemed to recover quite quickly. She was able to walk around the room without much pain.

The baby Elizabeth and the wet-nurse slept outside and spent most of the day with Mary who loved doting on her new child.

Elizabeth, who slowly gained a normal pinkish color and now took breaks between crying her lungs out, grew on Catherine.

"You were very brave, Catherine."

"It was one of the most frightening experiences I saw," Catherine said.

"It was well worth the effort. Bringing a new life into the world is an honor and a gift. I wouldn't trade it for anything in the world. Despite the dangers."

"And the pain?"

"The pain is forgotten as with everything in time," she assured her. "Love overwhelms the pain."

Before long, her mother was churched and could leave her confinement chamber. With that, Catherine returned to work in the dairy but tried to see her new sister in the afternoons every day. She felt a special connection to her.

After three months, her grandmother and grandfather arrived to be guests at Elizabeth's baptism.

The Godparents were William Stafford's sister and Sir Robert Bracken, who was their neighbor and good friend. They didn't have many friends to call upon to be Godparents but these would do just fine.

After the church ceremony there is a small dinner given at

the house. A pig was spit roasted especially for this occasion, and, alongside the pig, the table was filled with pies and other delicacies.

The arrival of autumn ushered in the harvest in Essex. The wheat had been harvested and was drying out in the fields as the apples and fruits ripened, ready to be picked. The cool weather also kept Catherine indoors. She found herself spending more time in the solar learning to spin yarn from the wool of their sheep.

She watched her younger sister Elizabeth while the wet-nurse rested and rocked her cradle with one foot.

As if there wasn't already enough reason to celebrate there was amazing news from London that sent the whole country into an uproar of celebration.

Queen Jane had given birth to a son! She had a difficult birth but had succeeded where others had failed.

"Mother, shall we go to London for the christening?" An event which was sure to be the grandest the Kingdom had seen.

"We won't be invited."

"But grandfather is at court."

"He is on the King's business. You forget that we are disgraced. No one would want us near the Prince."

Catherine sighed. It didn't seem fair but who was she to complain. Still, she was allowed to go with a chaperone to watch the bonfires being lit in the streets and celebrate with the others that the Kingdom had an heir.

Their happiness was cut short by the arrival of her grand-father who rode with his shoulders hunched. Looking more withdrawn than ever.

"What is the matter?" Mary had not wasted a moment to ask.

"The Queen has died and the court plunged into mourning."

"God rest her soul." Mary crossed herself and Catherine, who was watching the exchange, did the same. "But what ailed her?"

"She had childbed fever. The King was away at Greenwich and did not reach her before she passed. She will be buried at Westminster."

"And the Prince?"

"Healthy, or so they say. I have not seen him myself, of course. Edward Seymour was named Godfather. I don't think they'll delay the christening for long."

He didn't have to say the fear everyone held out loud. Before this Prince Edward, there had been two other sons who slept in the royal cradle, but they had both died young. Every breath this precious child took would be watched and examined. Catherine could imagine with every cough the country would hold its breath.

"The King? He must be devastated."

"He has secluded himself away in his rooms." Thomas Boleyn leaned in to whisper the words. "He has called for a chantry to be opened for her.

"But that is to return to Rome."

He shrugged, stepping away from his daughter.

"Catherine, why don't you see if my rooms are ready?"

Catherine knew this was to get her out of the way. She left them to walk around the estate in seclusion, but she quickly returned, knowing that his rooms were already cleaned and ready for use.

She stalked after them trying to see where they had gone in the rose garden. She hadn't intended to make herself known, but her mother was too used to her games and pulled away from her father when she heard the swish of her gown.

"Catherine, I hope you are not eavesdropping."

"Not at all, Mother." Catherine came around the bend, curtseying to both of them. "I came to tell you that your rooms are ready, Grandfather."

Thomas Boleyn smiled. "She's wasted here. What a good little spy she would make, keeping her head even when she is caught."

"All in due time. I would prefer she didn't pick up any unladylike habits though." Mary was scowling and Catherine looked down at the ground in shame.

She couldn't help herself sometimes.

Chapter Five

That Christmas they did not travel, as, yet again, Mary was with child. They brought in the Yule log at Rochford Hall and had a small party. On Christmas Day they sang carols, and Catherine danced for the family and played the lute.

For New Year's, they had a surprise visit from both Elizabeth and Thomas Boleyn who came with gifts. No one was expecting them, and the household rushed to clean out extra rooms to house the extra people.

Catherine quickly realized something was not quite right with her grandmother. All the other times she had seen her, she had been quick-witted and sharp with an insult or comment, but now she seemed demure. She also couldn't help notice the haphazard cough she seemed to have developed.

"It's just this weather," she explained to Mary who had also been concerned. "It comes and it goes."

"And this sudden visit?"

"I felt it was prudent to spend time with the remaining family I had."

"Even though I am such a disappointment?"

Catherine nearly choked on the warm ale she was drinking.

"Your failings are my own fault. I hope we can put that bad business aside."

"As you wish, Mother."

Despite the generous presents, Mary didn't seem to warm up too much to either of her parents. She was more than courteous to her mother, but she never seemed to regard her as more than an unwelcome guest. Catherine knew why but still thought the whole scene was incredibly sad considering how fragmented the family had become.

At length, her grandparents left and they were left to their own devices.

By spring, they received word that Elizabeth was not well at all. She had suffered through the long winter, but her cough had not mended with the arrival of warmer weather. She had grown weak and was surely lying on her deathbed.

Mary did not hesitate to travel to her side, even in her condition. Catherine came along to watch over her too.

Her grandmother was in a dark room, a fire was blazing in the fireplace making the room stifling hot. She was clutching at a crucifix as a lady-in-waiting sat by her side reading from the bible.

"Ah, my daughter." She coughed seeing Mary approaching.

Mary knelt by her bedside. "How are you feeling today?"

"Weak — like I cannot breath," came the raspy reply.

Catherine, who hung back by the door, was stunned by the change in the woman. It scared her more than sitting by her mother's bedside during her labor. She slunk out of the room before either of them would notice.

She found her grandfather in the dining hall, arguing with the cook over the cost of bacon. He had been wringing his hands together as he paced the rooms all day. The minute he noticed something displeasing, he would yell at the nearest person, so she had stayed out of his way.

"Grandfather, could I help you in some way?" Her soft voice seemed to pierce his anger-laden brain and he dismissed the cook.

"No, there is nothing for you to do. Shouldn't you be with your mother?"

"I thought I might keep you company. Perhaps a game of cards might distract you?"

He allowed her to lead him to a table and ordered for a pack of cards to be brought to them.

"Have you been to court?" Catherine asked as she shuffled the cards for a game of pique.

"Not since March. There is much discussion and debate on who the King will take next as his bride."

Her grandfather was quite open with her about things that he had heard. Perhaps knowing how she enjoyed hearing tales.

"Any idea who?"

"A French princess perhaps." He shrugged.

For once the King did not seem to have a suitable wife lined up to replace his last queen.

They played cards well into dinner time and ate together informally in the parlor until Mary joined them.

"How is your mother?" Thomas asked.

"Tired and weak. Has she seen a doctor?"

"Many, they recommended potions and herbs but none of their treatments helped. I fear she is drifting away from us." He went pale.

They could all see how downcast he was. Mary did a double take at the audible stress in his voice.

"We shall pray for her to get better."

However, their prayers were not answered, and, in April, she passed away.

Their household was dressed in black and they followed strict mourning for her. Mary worried for her own father and encouraged Harry and Catherine to spend time with him to try and bring up his spirits.

Catherine, who had not known her grandmother much, found herself saddened by the emptiness that seemed to hang over Hever Castle. Her own mother would have to reenter confinement soon, and that was a daunting task after the preparations for the funeral had seemed to sap everyone's strength and energy.

Finally, as Mary was nearing her time, Catherine had to encourage her mother to leave her childhood home to return to Rochford Hall.

"I'll ride ahead and guard you." Harry promised.

He was strutting around the hall, a hand on his empty scabbard. It was a ceremonial sword, and, since he was not allowed to carry it around, he had kept the scabbard close at hand. He was awfully proud to show off his fighting skills.

"Perhaps the King will go to war against France and I shall be his squire."

"The King wouldn't go to war against France," Catherine snapped at her brother's insensitivity.

"Why not?"

"He's looking to make an alliance with them or with the emperor. You would know that if you paid any attention."

"Pfft."

"That's enough," Mary said, trying to get them to settle down. "Bickering doesn't help me either."

Catherine looked chastised. Her brother was always infuriating, but she should really know better.

In the end their journey home was slow going as Mary was experiencing pain in her stomach.

"I should have left sooner," Mary said as Catherine held her hand.

Despite the comfort of the litter, Mary still winced with every bump in the road. When they finally arrived at Rochford Hall, Mary was carried up straight to bed and William called for a midwife and doctor to come see her.

Catherine was with her as the midwife poked and prodded her belly, listening as best she could.

"You might go into labor prematurely," she said. "You shouldn't move from the bed."

Mary didn't protest in her discomfort. Catherine was getting worried too. Would her mother die in childbed as the Queen had done? She didn't seem as strong as before, and her grandmother's death had not helped matters either.

In the end, the midwife's predictions were proven correct. At the end of the week Mary had gone into labor and delivered a baby boy. Catherine was by her side this time as well but was surprised by his small size, more than that the midwife had to struggle to help him breathe and he had coughed up bile.

She had heard the midwife tell the priest who had come that the baby's lungs were too weak and that he should urge the parent to baptize the child quickly. Catherine didn't repeat this to her mother. But she watched over her new brother with special attention, rocking him in her own arms.

He wasn't like Elizabeth at all, who had begun toddling

around in the nursery. He had trouble latching on to the wet-nurse and Catherine tried to coax him to suck on a piece of linen dipped in goat's milk. Everyone seemed to know but no one dared to admit that this child was slipping away slowly. Before the end of the week, he was baptized William for his father.

Each morning Catherine woke and anxiously went to check his cradle, only breathing a sigh of relief when she saw he was breathing his little raspy breaths. But after a month, she awoke to cries from the nurse.

Little William had died in the night.

Mary was distraught and took to her bed. Catherine was both shocked and grieved like never before, but she couldn't take to her bed. With her mother sick with grief, she had to care for her and help manage the rest of the household in her place.

That spring she jumped headfirst into the responsibilities of an adult. Her younger sister needed attention now that Mary was incapacitated, the kitchen and the garden needed to be looked after, and the servants needed to be instructed on their tasks.

Catherine had known something was amiss from the moment a liveried servant had practically fallen from his horse. She had been watching from the window as the steward spoke to him and upon hearing the news ushered him inside quickly.

She didn't have time to say anything to her mother as the man entered not long after. His sullen expression speaking volumes. William stood in front of Mary as if guarding her from the bad news. They watched in silence as the servant took off his cap and told them that his master Thomas Boleyn was dead.

To her credit Mary didn't faint or flinch.

"Thank you for telling us. You can eat in the kitchens. We shall set out for Hever today."

Catherine followed her mother out of the room. She kept waiting for her to cry or show some sort of emotion, but she remained stoic to the point where Catherine wasn't sure if her mother loved her father or cared for him.

When she was older, perhaps she would have realized this as shutting herself off from the world. Grief was wounding Mary, and, in order to escape it, she would try to pretend like it didn't exist.

So, yet again, the family was plunged into mourning.

Thomas Boleyn's funeral was a relatively simple ceremony. The family was decked from head to toe in black along with the servants; a few carried his coat of arms and banners before them as the church bells rang. The men of the family and household were given specially made black staves to carry. William was one of those honored to carry the casket to its final resting place. They arranged themselves to walk towards the graveyard.

Despite the hints of early spring, the procession appeared to Catherine to be a black cloud of misery encroaching upon the church.

Thomas's will became another issue. Rochford Hall now passed to Mary, but Hever Castle reverted back to the King. They could keep his personal possessions, and, after his outstanding bills were paid, then they would have the bulk of the remainder of his fortune too.

Catherine had inherited a few pieces from her grandmother. A pearl brooch, a gold necklace with a ruby pendant, and a pair of gloves trimmed with sable. Her mother had promised to have some of her dresses recut for her as well in newer fashions.

As for Thomas Boleyn, there was nothing for her to keep. In fact, most of it was given to William or her brother, Harry. His horses would be brought back to Rochford Hall.

There was nothing joyous about this new fortune though. Cromwell's men had arrived swiftly to appraise the castle and ensure nothing was taken that belonged to the King now. Mary had even left the portraits, not wishing to have the reminder. Catherine saw how she clung to William in the months that followed her father's death as if she feared she would lose him too.

The other thing Catherine learned was that despite the tragedies that seemed to come on in quick succession, life went on. It had to.

Catherine had an easy summer as her mother seemed to have no time for her. But this came to an abrupt end with the news that her uncle was going to be paying a formal visit in two months. Her mother was on edge the minute she saw the liveried servant from the Duke of Norfolk. It was enough to put the rest of the household in a state of unrest.

Everyone worked with their heads down, trying to stay out of her way and finish with their new tasks. Mary demanded the new rushes be finished by the time they arrived. In an effort to escape some other more arduous task, Catherine went with the women and spent long days outside. She helped as best she could, weaving the weeds into plaits to be sewn together. Several mats were already completed, but many more would be required to replace the ones in the house.

Sometimes she said she was going out to work with them but instead snuck away to sit by the river, relaxing in the shade. Of course, when she was discovered, she regretted her lazy behavior. Mary did not bother with the stick but put her to work gathering herbs to be dried.

So Catherine spent hours bent over in the gardens, cutting away at plants. Her inexperienced hands getting stung by the thorns and little spikes of various plants until a kind woman handed her a pair of gloves.

"It's best you don't ruin your hands," she said.

For her part, Catherine sulked — couldn't she be one of those ladies who did nothing but sew, dance, read, and relax all day?

Only her brother seemed adept at avoiding hard tasks. He was always out hunting and fishing most days and with his tutors.

A week or so before the arrival of the Duke and his retinue, the laundry was done. In big vats, they boiled the linen with soap and then wrung it out. Lines were set up on a sunny day for the linen to be dried.

Finally, the old rushes were taken out and the floors swept and scrubbed as best as possible. Catherine's only joy was the smell of the fresh herbs she had dried being strewn about the floors to be then covered by the rush mats.

The household and county was rewarded for all of its work when their glorious visitor finally rode up the road through Rochford Hall's gatehouse. Catherine stood behind her mother as her uncle rode into their courtyard. She watched his hawk-like gaze critically sweep over them. Catherine noted how he seemed to look down his nose at them as if they weren't worth his time and he had been inconvenienced by having to visit.

If only he knew how inconvenienced she had been by his

visit. The thought almost made her giggle but she kept herself in check. This was one of the most powerful men in the Kingdom with one of the largest land holdings, whereas they were just his disgraced relatives. She was not permitted to laugh or even make a sound.

He greeted first William, who had put on his best suit, and then turned to give the rest a graceful nod in acknowledgement.

Dinner was served in the great hall, and, despite the heaps of food on the table and the liberal amounts of wine being served, the room was quieter than usual. The presence of the Duke put everyone on their best behavior. No one spoke too loudly and tried not to belch. Catherine saw her mother motion to the musicians to fill the silence with a song. Norfolk was unimpressed by all of this, of course, he was used to grandeur.

Finally, after the end of the meal that seemed to drag on for hours, Catherine was excused alongside the other children, as the adults would retreat into a private room for a family conference.

Catherine did not do as she was told. She was too curious to try not to listen. Instead of walking to her room, she doubled back and went to the library where there was a grate she had found and could overhear them speaking in the private office.

She glanced around the dark room, making sure no one was around. She was sure no one knew of this little spot. She had stumbled across it by accident herself when she was chasing a dog around the room that had stolen her hair ribbon. She had knelt down to pick up the fallen ribbon when she discovered it.

The grate was hers — she shared it with no one, not even her brother, and it made her feel giddy to have such a secret.

Now Catherine crouched down and listened to the voices of her family intently.

"I have written to Jane." Her uncle's deep voice was the first thing she heard.

"We cannot trust that spiteful..." Catherine's mother was silenced — she could picture her stepfather putting a steady hand over her mother's.

"She will work for the family, and I do have a plan, an alternative to make sure Jane will do what she has promised," her uncle continued.

The silence that followed was filled with anticipation as the rest waited to hear what he had the say.

"Catherine shall be placed in the Queen's new household."

"No!" Her mother's gasp covered Catherine's own. "I mean, surely she is not ready for such a task and the King is still in mourning — he can't be looking for a wife already."

"On the contrary, he is looking, and whoever he settles on will be served by those in our household."

"If Cromwell has his way, then the King will marry a German Protestant," the Duke said. "But the King prefers a French princess." He paused to take a drink before continuing. "Regardless, both Jane and Catherine will be placed strategically and it will advance this family's fortunes."

Catherine sat back on her heels — years ago it had been her dream to join the court and be one of those blessed ladies who served the Queen and danced with handsome knights and chevaliers. But now the Tower superseded every thought of pleasure. Those drafty rooms would never be wiped from her memory.

However, she wouldn't be going to the Tower this time, and if she was careful and well behaved, she would never see the inside of the Tower again either. With this thought she leaned in again to listen.

"What will we do?" Thomas Howard said.

"Nothing, of course. We'll play our cards right until the right time."

Catherine wasn't sure what they were referring to.

"I can see it is getting late — we shall retire for now — I shall keep you abreast of any developments."

Catherine got to her feet at those words and made her way back to her rooms as quickly as possible before she was caught.

The next day, when she was called into her mother's solar, she tried to hold back the excitement at the news she knew she would be receiving.

Instead she was surprised with a lecture.

"I have let you run incredibly wild and it is probably making you irresponsible. I know how you like to run off if no one is watching you. Finding you by the river instead of sewing rushes is just one of the many complaints I've been hearing about you."

"Lady Mother?!" Catherine began protesting but was stopped by the glare she received.

"I am putting you to work in the dairy."

"I am not milking cows."

"I wouldn't trust you to milk a cow," her mother said. The snap in her voice made Catherine wince. She was sounding like a spoiled child. "You shall learn how to run a dairy, and, if it means getting your hands dirty once in a while, you will have to do it. This shall be your responsibility now."

"I don't know anything about the dairy." Yet again, this was the wrong thing to say as her mother's eyes narrowed.

"You shall learn. There is more to life than wasting away

your days." Mary sent her away without a word about going to court. Catherine would much rather think about dresses and dances than cows. Perhaps something had changed and her uncle decided against sending her to court.

Not knowing what to do, she returned to her room and sat on her bed, pulling at some threads in her embroidery. It wasn't long before she was interrupted from her sulking by her maid coming in and telling her the steward was waiting for her downstairs.

He escorted her to the north side of the manor to the dairy — going over what was needed of her. The manor could afford to have several cows to maintain a constant production of milk, butter and cheese. These were all things that they ate on a daily basis. Some they sent to the King's kitchens as a gift, and another portion they sold at the market or used to pay servants.

Catherine tried to make a mental note of this but their walk was brief.

"One of my daughters is also working in the dairy. She will see you are looked after. Your Lady mother wishes you to work in the dairy after church in the morning until supper in the evening. She will let you know when she has other tasks for you," he said.

Catherine knew it was futile to complain and stepped inside the dairy. The first thing she noticed was the strong smell of fermenting milk that had been left to sit overnight. The building itself was situated on the north side of the house where the dairy could be covered by the shade and never be in direct sunlight. The floor was made up of stone tile, and what looked like a steady stream of water was passing through the left side of the building.

Catherine took in the baskets, linen and stoneware. There

were countless other tools that she had no idea what they were there for.

When the two other maids saw her they curtseyed low and introduced themselves.

"I am Silvia, I am just learning myself."

"My name is Angela, Mistress Catherine."

A third girl walked in carrying a fresh pail of milk. "And my name is Doris."

"Pleasure to meet you all."

The girls hid a snigger at her formality, but Catherine really wasn't sure how to begin.

Doris, who seemed to be in charge of the group, decided to speak first. "Perhaps you would like to be shown what we do?"

Catherine nodded.

"Well, first every morning we go milk the cows in the barn. On a good day you'll get a big pail like this." She pointed to the one she carried in. "But don't worry we won't send you to the barn your ladyship." The others sniggered.

"I am not afraid of the barn you know."

"Didn't mean to suggest you were."

"So if we make butter, we pour some milk into one of these." She pointed to a large stone pot. "And the next day all the cream will rise to the top and we collect it. Then we have to churn it until you hear a wet sort of sound and use the wood paddles to press out all the milk from it leaving us with butter that we have to salt."

Catherine was a bit stunned by all the work but let her continue.

"For cheese, we need renette."

"What is renette?"

"Comes from the stomach of a young lamb."

Catherine blanched at the thought, making the woman laugh. "Where do you think your dinner comes from?"

"But touching it and killing it…" That would be appalling.

"You need to toughen up, besides you won't be doing any slaughtering but you did ask what it was." Doris shrugged.

"So we separate out the whey and then let the milk curdle in the cheese cloth. The most important thing I can tell you is that everything needs to be clean."

Catherine nodded. At least that she could understand.

Doris tapped the floor with her heel. "We regularly pour cold water on the stone. The stone soaks it up and keeps the room cool. It's hard to keep the temperature down in the summer, but you'll find it pleasant in here even when it's scorching out there."

"Angela can show you how to salt butter — that's what you can do for now."

"I thought I was in charge." Catherine didn't like feeling like she was being ordered around.

Doris gave her a poignant look. "What shall we do then?"

Catherine was defeated; she didn't know enough to give any orders. "Well I can keep the records…"

"The steward does that. He comes in and weighs and measures everything we produce. I suppose you can help him with that."

"So I'll salt butter."

"That's the spirit."

Angela was much friendlier than Doris.

"Don't fret too much about Doris. She's been running the dairy for ages," she said as she showed Catherine how to measure out the precious salt.

"Just work it into the butter with the paddles. If you use your hands the butter would melt. It should solidify like that piece over there and that's when you'll know you are finished. Is that okay, Mistress Catherine?"

"Yes, I think I have the hang of it." Catherine took up the wooden paddles in her hands.

"You might want to wear an apron." Doris called over her shoulder as she was dumping cream into the churn.

Angela grabbed her one hanging on a peg by the door. "You don't want to stain your pretty dress."

Catherine looked down. This was one of her every day dresses but compared to what the girls were wearing it was very fine indeed.

The day passed by quickly with all the work she was given. They wouldn't let her do any of the more menial tasks for which Catherine was grateful, but working the butter was hard work for now. She knew her arms would be sore tomorrow. Luckily, as the sun was setting, she knew it must be time for supper and hung up her apron for the day

It surprised her that she was so proud of the butter she had set into molds.

She knew she must have smelled and the work had also left her sweaty, so she did her best to wash her hands and neck with some scented water from her rooms before heading down to dinner.

Her brother was ready with jokes and insults.

"You smell, Cathy!" He laughed holding his nose. "I think you should eat down there with the servants."

"Hush, Harry." Mary chided him.

William gave Catherine a warm smile. "You are learning important work. The dairy is just one of the many things that keeps this manor on its feet."

Catherine was too tired to complain or ask to be released from the work. This wasn't a fight she was willing to have at the moment. She sat down as lady-like as possible and ate as fast as she could without looking like she was shoveling food down her throat.

Harry was content only for a while and soon tried to rile her up some more. When she was watching, he dropped a knife full of butter on the ground.

"Oops. I guess you'll have to go make more butter, Cathy." But his joke was rewarded with a chuff to the back of his head by William. Even her younger sister Anne had frowned at him.

"Since when is wasting food and making fun of your sister part of the chivalric code? You shall not go riding tomorrow," their mother declared. "I honestly don't know when the both of you started misbehaving so much."

"I haven't done anything," Catherine muttered under her breath, but luckily her mother didn't hear.

———————

By the end of summer, Catherine had managed to learn a lot more about the dairy. That feeling of satisfaction at the end of the day only got better. She put aside her displeasure and focused on the work itself.

She was now able to make white cheese herself and knew how to churn butter, although this was her least favorite task. She helped the steward keep track of the records and ordered salt when supplies were running low. So while she still took every opportunity she had to sit by the river and read, she no longer felt working in dairy was such a struggle.

The world never stayed the same for too long, though. In October, just as the harvest was beginning, a messenger arrived from the court with a formal invitation for Lady Catherine Carey to take up her post as Lady-in-Waiting to the new Queen of England.

Catherine had remained silent beyond accepting it and thanking the messenger until he disappeared.

Her mother was ready for her questions when she turned to her.

"So it's true? I'm going to court?"

"Yes, I have ordered gowns made for you."

"You have?"

"They should arrive within the next few days, and I shall have to see you packed and ready to leave within the month. I am sure the ladies are all pouring into court now."

"And who is the Queen? Who is he marrying?" Catherine had not heard yet.

"He's marrying Anne of Cleaves, she's making her way over to England now."

"Another Queen Anne?" Catherine gaped.

Mary nodded, looking away. "Well, we shall have a lot to discuss. You don't have to spend all day in the dairy anymore. You'll need to practice your dancing."

"I'll work there in the mornings. I'm helpful."

Catherine saw her mother raise an eyebrow but agreed.

After the gowns had arrived and her mother had her fitted to them, she took her for a walk in the gardens.

"You are going to court for several reasons, but the most important is that you are to serve your family."

"How?"

"With your eyes and ears — mostly." She smiled. "Your uncle needs you to keep an eye on Jane Rochford and report to him anything you hear."

"What would I hear?"

"Anything you think is important. It could be that the King had a fight with the Queen or with one of his advisors. It could be silly such as the King flirting with someone. Basically, anything that pertains to the King, Queen, the King's advisor, Lady Mary or any of our family you are to report to him."

"I shall be a spy?" Catherine's eyes gleamed.

"No, of course not. Goodness you should not be so excited by such a thing. You are there to serve the Queen. Only if you happen to overhear something you are to report it. That's what your uncle would like."

"And you?

"I would prefer you stay as far from the court as possible. There are too many ways for a young girl to get caught up in trouble."

Her mother went rigid as if she had been struck. She peered down at her, taking hold of her hands. She looked as though she was trying to see into Catherine's very soul.

"You won't dance and flirt with young handsome men. It would be unseemly."

"I won't dance unless I have to," Catherine promised. "I'll be the living embodiment of modesty."

"Good. If I or your uncle hear any rumors about you, then you will be taken away from court."

"I have no interest in men," Catherine repeated. That much was true. She tended to avoid Harry these days. Him and his friends were annoying and tedious.

"And Lady Rochford? What am I supposed to be watching her for?" Catherine suddenly remembered.

"Just that she is reporting everything and not whispering with other people about family secrets."

Catherine was a bit confused.

"I warned you before about her. She is a vile cunning woman and you cannot trust her. But you also cannot take your eyes off of her either, or who knows what trouble she will cause. Just make sure she is not up to some sort of trouble, understood?"

"Yes, Lady Mother."

Although Catherine was not very clear at all about what she was supposed to be watching out for. What trouble would she be causing?

"It's important to keep things to yourself too. Don't repeat what you hear to anyone but your uncle. Information is powerful."

Catherine nodded. She knew this already.

It was not long before the country was filled with rumors about the new queen. Reports had come in saying that she was gracious and beautiful. There were other reports too that she had been the King's only option since none of the French Princesses would have him.

Catherine didn't blame them.

As the Queen's retinue was nearing Calais, she would meet with the other ladies at Westminster then travel with them to Calais to greet the Queen and begin serving her.

Her trunk of dresses and her two new gowns were packed away. Her mother gave her instructions up until the last possible moment.

"Mother, I shall be fine." Catherine was getting anxious to leave just to escape her mother's insistent warnings and advice.

"Mary, she will be alright." William, her stepfather, appeared at his wife's side, taking her arm.

"Be safe," Mary said.

Those were the last words Catherine heard as she was helped on her horse and began the journey to London.

Chapter Six

✦❧❧❦✦

Being safe would be easy, or so Catherine thought. Being a good lady-in-waiting would be another thing entirely. She hoped beyond hope that she wouldn't embarrass herself.

The city was larger than Catherine remembered it, perhaps because the last time she had journeyed through they had rushed through the main street, up to the palace. That had been several years ago.

She kept her gaze purposefully away from the direction of the Tower of London. She had spied its crenellations and immediately recognized it. It was like an ever-present threat looming over everyone. She didn't know how they could bear it.

In the courtyard, stable boys leapt up to help her from her horse, and she gave her letter of invitation to a porter who escorted her to the Queen's rooms, promising that her trunks would follow her too.

Since the Queen had not taken up residence yet, there were no guards posted on the doors, nor did she need a formal introduction. Besides a brief hesitation, she entered the double doors.

A very different sight greeted her from what she imagined. Several unknown ladies were perched around the room, chatting away in tight knit groups. Others were playing cards, while the new arrivals were trying to get themselves settled.

They all looked her way as she entered. A vaguely familiar face approached her in the awkward silence that ensued.

"Ah! This is my beautiful niece Catherine Carey."

"Lady Rochford." Catherine curtseyed coolly, identifying her aunt.

It made her laugh. "There's no need for such formality between family, is there?" And pulled her into a hug.

"I'll introduce you to everyone."

Lady Rutland was the first to step forward. She was a senior lady at court, and, besides her own aunt, the most seasoned — having served two queens previously.

After introductions were concluded, Catherine was told she would be sharing a room with the younger ladies of the household, including a cousin of hers, Katherine Howard.

"This shall make things difficult," Katherine Howard pouted. "I wanted to be the only Katherine."

Catherine was taken aback by such silliness. "Well I am Catherine Carey, and you are a Howard. That's quite different. You can call me Cate if you want."

"Oh that's ever so nice. At least I won't ever forget your name!" Katherine said, giggling. "It's so hard to remember everyone's name. I never expected the court to be filled with so many people! And such handsome gentlemen everywhere you look. You haven't been to dinner but you will see. You can call me Kitty if you want, although I prefer Katherine, it is much more becoming."

Catherine smiled. She was getting the impression that her cousin, though close in age to her, was too foolish and silly for her tastes. Unfortunately, four ladies would be sleeping in this room, and, since there was hardly any space in the palace, this would not change any time soon.

Katherine escaped before long, wanting to find some sort of amusement. Catherine sat on her bed, wishing to sleep for a moment after the long journey.

Before they had to dress for dinner, she let her cousin show her around. It was rare to find an empty corridor and people always seemed to be running around, doing something important.

There were more servants in the kitchens alone than there had been in all of Rochford Hall. She had always thought her old home was a grand place, but it was nothing when compared to Westminster. This wasn't even the greatest of the King's residences.

The palace, the people — as Catherine was taking it all in, she knew her eyes were wide with amazement, her stride jerky and uncertain. They had just begun.

The castle ran like clockwork — an army of servants followed a grueling schedule to ensure that everything was precisely as the King wished it to be. It varied sometimes, but there was always something that needed to be cleaned, a fire to be stoked, a roast to be marinated.

Rules for how this was to be done governed the lives of both the courtiers and the servants alike. You couldn't just do things when you wanted to. Dinner was served at an appointed time. The King would go hunting at a certain hour, and if you were late you were out of luck.

Finally, they returned to the Queen's rooms. Catherine was trying to puzzle out how she would ever be able to keep track of all of this when Katherine came in to change for dinner. She followed suit and changed into one of her finer gowns. It was one of her favorites. A warm burgundy bodice and skirt trimmed with black fur that revealed the petticoat beneath. The petticoat she picked was embroidered with a pattern of squares containing images of birds and flowers alternating between black and red silk.

She followed the other ladies and took up her seat in the great hall — a table set out especially for the ladies and maids in waiting. It was a place of honor due to its closeness to the great dais where the King and Queen would eat.

The court did not have to wait long for the King to make his appearance. With a flourish the trumpeters announced his arrival and they all stood.

She watched with near horror as the King entered and took his seat beneath the cloth of estate. It had been a long time since she had last seen him, so she was surprised to find he had changed so much. He seemed to have doubled in size.

"Look at the brooch in his hat!" Katherine whispered in her ear. "I would do anything for ruby of that size."

Catherine shook her head. She hadn't been able to look past his jowls.

She also learned she would have to pace herself, as dish after dish was brought into the Hall.

The King ate from everything with a ferocious appetite calling for more wine and more food. Occasionally, he would send a dish to some of his favorites dining below. Once he had eaten his fill, he called for some music and dancing.

Catherine watched his eyes turning towards their table. His gaze focused on hers for a moment as if he recognized her but couldn't quite place her. Catherine looked away; there was no need to draw the attention of her unacknowledged father. By her side Kitty was shifting in her seat, then suddenly looked down with a giggle.

"What is it?" Catherine asked.

"Did you see the King look at me?" she said. "Perhaps he will ask me for a dance."

"Hardly likely." Another girl interjected as she sat up straighter preening herself. "He would rather choose me than a silly little girl like you."

Catherine could see Kitty ready to jump out at her and grabbed her hand under the table.

The King indeed danced with them. First he chose Lady Rutland, then took Kitty out for a quick jig. Catherine could see how he tried to hide the wince of pain as he did some of the more complicated moves.

He laughed when the dance was over, covering up the fact he was left so out of breath.

"I should rest and save myself for my beautiful betrothed. But continue dancing for us ladies." He all but hobbled back to his great seat.

Catherine saw how everyone pretended to have seen nothing. This was how the game was played.

Kitty did not return to her seat. Several gentlemen vied for her attention — after all, she was a striking beauty with her blonde hair and dark eyes. More than that, she was flirtatious and inviting. Catherine did not know how she managed it nor who had taught her to act this coquettishly. Was she not concerned about her reputation?

She was surprised to feel a pang of jealousy at the attention her younger cousin was getting, but, at the same time, she was more concerned with blending in and remaining anonymous in this court. Bringing attention upon herself was dangerous.

By the time she reached her bed, it was after midnight. They would begin their travels to Rochford then to Calais provided the sea was calm. A fleet of ships was being prepared to accompany them to the new Queen.

———————————————

"Girls, wake up!"

A loud shout made Catherine jump in her bed. She blinked away the confusion and focused her sight on the woman in the doorway. Lady Brown was there with her hands on her hips, looking displeased.

"You were up too late dancing around. This will teach you to go to bed at an appropriate time."

Catherine could hear Kitty giggling in the bed beside her.

"Well get up and dress — we are to leave soon, and if you aren't ready then you shall be left behind."

The girls all leapt out of bed. There was a lot of digging around trunks and scrambling to get dressed as they took turns lacing each other into their sleeves and petticoats. Servants filed in after each had left and packed away their trunks to be carried along with them to their destination.

Catherine was one of the first out of the rooms, dressed in a dark green gown suitable for riding, as it wouldn't show the dirt on the hem as much and the thick material would keep her warm. Around her neck was the pearl necklace her mother had given her.

She had seen Kitty eyeing it when she had taken it out of its locked case. She didn't think she had too much in the way of possessions, but she supposed she had more than Kitty.

With the ladies assembled, they set out towards a court-yard where a select group of Lords and Gentlemen had arranged themselves with their households. Catherine was given a horse from the King's stable to ride and a groom cupped his hands together to help her leap into the saddle.

He gave her a smile, but she flushed and looked away, ignoring him. She wasn't a giggly chit like Kitty.

Around them, carts filled with goods would be traveling, as well as a retinue of yeomen to act as their guards, although no one would be foolish enough to attack a band of the King's.

The King himself would be following on later. Their official meeting place was set to be Greenwich.

Catherine, who had never traveled with a court even one as small as this, was flustered by all the activity. But luckily, she had the older ladies to follow and took up a spot behind Lady Rochford who had been just as cold to her as she had been to her after their first encounter.

All day they traveled at a slow pace until they reached the first inn on the roadside.

It was Lady Brown who arranged all the sleeping arrangements, and Catherine found herself crammed into a bed with two other girls. She did not sleep much on the journey. When they finally arrived at Rochester Castle, they were housed and fed well.

It was the first time she was given an opportunity to bathe properly, and, after tipping a manservant a penny, she received a bucket of deliciously hot water and a clean towel.

The next day, a select few ladies assembled to embark for Calais. Catherine was pleased to have been selected, where Kitty had been overlooked. Already, she had developed a mischievous reputation that would not be welcomed on this important meeting.

Catherine had never traveled by ship before and was anxious about the journey. She thought it would be similar to traveling by barge, but, after the ship disembarked, she felt her legs nearly give out as the waves began rocking the boat.

Some of the ladies had gone beneath deck to what would

be the Queen's rooms, but she had remained on deck. Now she regretted not going. Perhaps it would be better beneath deck.

The ship went over a particularly large wave and she reached out her hand to grasp something. That something turned out to be a young man who had been running by.

They blinked at each other.

"I apologize, sir." Catherine took her hand away from his shoulder. He was looking at her, considering.

"You don't have your sea legs yet." He offered her his arm to steady her.

She wasn't going to take it; after all, they hadn't been introduced.

"The ship is going to rock again, and I'm afraid you will fall."

Stoutly, she took his hand, and he led her to the side of the ship.

"And may I have your name?" he asked.

"Catherine Carey, I am a maid-in-waiting to the new Queen."

"Ah, well I am Francis Knollys, gentleman usher."

"And rescuer of damsels in distress?"

This made him laugh. They reached the balustrade and she gripped it, letting go of his arm.

"If you feel sick, just lean over and try to avoid the deck and your pretty dress."

Catherine flushed with embarrassment, but he was gone from her side to carry out whatever job he had been in the middle of.

Indeed, she had been sick not long after his departure, and she was glad that Francis hadn't been around to see. As she wiped the corner of her mouth with a handkerchief, she thanked her lucky stars that she had eaten a light breakfast.

She hadn't gotten a good look at Francis, but she knew he was a good head taller than herself and had light blonde hair. She would thank him if she got the opportunity, but, given his flirtatious comment, she was hesitant to run into him again.

For all she knew he was married!

The journey was blissfully short. Catherine learned that today the sea had been calm, and she was even more embarrassed by her terrible reaction.

"I saw you on deck with that handsome young man." Madge was in line at her side as the ladies assembled to walk off the ship. The dock was strangely empty, as most people had gathered at the gates of Calais to catch a glimpse of the Lady Anne as she entered the city.

The ladies moved quickly through the streets and entered the palace, where they assembled along with the gentlemen to wait for the Anne of Cleves to arrive. From the noise outside, they did not have to wait long. There was great cheering, and it was clear that she had already gained favor with the people.

The room seemed to hold its breath in anticipation.

Then, just as suddenly, she had entered the room. A retinue of German lords and ladies at her heels. There was a pause as the English courtiers took in her strange dress and heavy headgear. In the next moment, they were bowing low, and, after she took her seat set up on a dais, Lord Lisle at her side, everyone stood waiting to be introduced.

It became clear very quickly that she could barely speak any English. Her German translator was constantly murmuring in her ear, and she seemed dazed by all the new faces and names.

Then it was time for her ladies to be introduced to her, and Catherine watched as her eyes went wide as Jane Boleyn's name was said. She must have heard all the tales about Anne.

Would it surprise her to learn that several of her cousins were going to be serving her?

Catherine came forward when her name was finally called and curtseyed low.

"P-pleasure t-to meet you." The lady stumbled over the words, but it was a better attempt than what she had managed earlier. Anne extended her hand and Catherine kissed it, promising to serve her loyally.

As she stepped away, Catherine felt a sense of pity for her. She didn't know what she would have done if she had been presented at a German court.

After everyone was presented, Lady Anne announced in her thick German accent that she wished to retire. The ladies fell into step behind her with Lady Lisle taking her husband's place at her side and showed her where she could rest until they departed.

The plan was to leave before nightfall, so she wouldn't be able to rest for long. Catherine didn't think she knew that.

Lady Anne seemed sweet, if not a bit naïve as she wondered at the other servants present in her rooms. These were ladies and gentlemen hired from the lower rungs of nobility to serve her. They would look after her rooms, keep a fire lit, clean and a variety of other tasks.

Perhaps she had never been served by so many people before. Catherine could relate, being new to court herself, but she had been better prepared. She promised herself she would try to help her in any way she could.

Lady Anne was looking from one person to another, she looked lost as to what she could do. Lady Rochford had told her that they would be departing soon but that she could rest in bed if she wished or hear some music. Lady Anne nodded and took a seat by the window, this wasn't the chair meant for her but the other ladies moved their chairs around so they faced her.

Lutes were brought in and Catherine, along with some of the other ladies, strung up a tune they had been taught.

"The King composed this," Lady Rochford said loud enough for everyone to hear.

"It very good," Anne said.

Catherine was on alert though, sensing a trap. Jane looked too pleased with herself.

"Yes, he wrote it for Anne Boleyn."

Several twangs were heard as the women missed the strings before resuming, trying to pretend as though nothing had happened. To her credit, Anne of Cleves did not blanch or complain. She just repeated herself very forcibly.

"It very good."

Lady Rochford seemed put out by her inability to incite any reaction from her. She settled on a different tactic and was all but friendly to her.

On the journey back to England, Catherine was prepared and ready with a hand on the railing as the ship set off.

The crowds of people watching them get on board made her watch the way she walked and she kept a smile until she was well out of sight. Anne seemed to have an easier time with the crowds; they only wanted a wave and a smile from her, which she could easily do. In contrast, the courtiers were much more demanding.

Now that Anne was here, Catherine couldn't go gallivanting around the deck or do as she pleased. It was her duty to be by her mistress's side until she was released.

In the rooms, they discovered that Anne was a fan of playing cards, and the ladies taught her how to play Primero since it was similar to a game she already knew. To win, a person needed to get four of a kind or a variety of different pairs. It was played between two people so they took turns playing against Anne, while the others advised her.

A knock at the door and a squire popped his head in. "We are nearly there."

"So soon!" Anne exclaimed. "This great fun." Pointing to the cards.

The ladies smiled and nodded.

Catherine saw Kitty whispering behind her sleeve to another of the maids and from the giggling it was nothing nice. She nudged her cousin harshly.

———

The arrival in Rochester managed to leave Lady Anne gaping in amazement at the great house and the pavilions set up with tableaus in her honor. Catherine thought that Cleves must not be a very rich nation if Anne, the sister of the Duke, found Rochester extravagant.

Rochester was the palace of the Archbishop, and it was one of his more old fashioned homes. They wouldn't be here long before continuing on to Blackheath.

With the ladies settled down, Lady Brown informed Anne of the events tomorrow.

"We arranged a few entertainments for you, as it is the New Year tomorrow. If it would please you, Lady Anne."

"It w-would." She nodded after her German lady translated for her.

"Good, good." Lady Brown smiled a bit helplessly. "You young ladies should retire, I don't want anyone to sleep in tomorrow." She had turned to look at them.

In their room, there was a lot of giggling and mocking of the Queen-to-Be.

"Would you like card?" Madge tried, mimicking her accent.

Only Catherine didn't find this amusing. They went on to comment on her gown, and the way she seemed to be so clumsy and dull.

Finally the girls climbed under the sheets and fell asleep. Catherine's thoughts were whirling for the poor girl who was only a couple years older than herself. She stood up and decided to go sit by the burning embers of the fireplace outside.

She opened the door but then quickly stopped in her tracks. Two figures were sitting by the fire, already talking in confidence. From the headdress of the woman on the right, she could tell was Jane Boleyn. Catherine looked behind her, making sure the others were asleep and, leaving the door cracked open, tried to listen to what they were saying.

"I told my husband that they would make a poor match, but he refuses to say anything to the King."

"He might like her after all." That was Jane.

"Perhaps... but I think you know as much as I do the likelihood of that happening. She is sweet enough but the King will not be satisfied with that. If she had a few months before the marriage, perhaps she could be taught more English and her dresses could be changed, but, as she is now, she is doomed to become a laughingstock."

"Those can be dangerous assumptions."

"It's the truth." Catherine finally recognized Lady Lisle's voice. "But you are right. Cromwell arranged this marriage — he won't like it if anyone steps in the way of his plans."

"No," Jane agreed. "It's better if we sit back and wait."

Catherine bit her lip, was it really better to sit back? She thought of how out of place Anne had seemed. She closed the door quietly, seeing that Lady Lisle had stood up.

Slinking back to her bed, she wondered what she could do. She didn't dare warn Anne — she didn't want to be interfering with court politics so soon. Especially not when those older than her seemed so hesitant to do so.

An idea struck her then. Perhaps she could make some effort to learn German and ingratiate herself to Anne that way. Then she could better communicate with her as well.

The next day, with the promised entertainment to look forward to, everyone took their time getting ready. Catherine selected the burgundy gown she wore at her first dinner at court. The fur would keep her warm in this drafty castle.

Anne was helped to wash and dress by some of the English ladies, as many of her German ladies had left after escorting her to Calais.

The gown she wore was another German creation. The ladies had attempted to prevent her from wearing the thick undercoat and the wide hoop skirt that created that unattractive bell figure. They also told her she didn't need to wear the cloth shirt up to her neckline, but Anne had looked horrified at the thought of being so exposed.

The English ladies exchanged glances. There was nothing wrong with modesty, but Anne was dressed more like a nun than a Queen.

They even showed her their own dresses, which were perfectly acceptable. Except Kitty Howard, who had done away with the scarf tucked into the neckline leaving her bust quite exposed when she curtseyed.

Still they went to hear mass and Anne's translator for once stopped translating. She did not speak Latin. Anne had been perturbed by what she must have seen as very Pope-ish customs. While Henry had broken away from Rome, he had not exactly embraced Protestantism either.

Catherine had to give her credit for not speaking out or

saying anything. She knew how important it was to hold your tongue. Anything contradictory to the King's wishes could be seen as treason.

After they listened to the sermon, they feasted on mince-meat pies and drank claret. Anne seemed quite pleased with the food, exclaiming over and over again that she had never eaten so well before.

Finally, they were taken to the hall where they were given seats by the great windows. Down below in the courtyard, a bull baiting had been set up. The dogs were barking incessantly, causing the bull in the courtyard to paw at the ground with his hoof and bellow.

Catherine looked away, she hated blood sports. Even jousting held little excitement for her. The sight of blood and danger made her sick to her stomach. So instead of focusing on the courtyard, she looked around the hall. She noticed several newcomers who had stayed behind with the King.

She wasn't experienced enough to suspect anything though and turned away when she heard Anne's cheerful exclamation.

The bull baiting was beginning. The dogs were let loose in the courtyard and they surrounded the bull. The younger ones were braver and leapt forward to snap at the bull but lost their courage the minute he tossed his horns in their direction.

Catherine knew this dance would continue for a long time.

Anne clapped loudly when the beast was felled and the dogs were carried away. All the excitement and blood had left those watching with adrenaline rushing through them.

Catherine, who avoided looking at the blood, noticed the crowd near a doorway move aside to let a man through. There was no mistaking the bulky form of the King, but he wasn't wearing his Kingly clothes — instead, as Catherine had been told he liked to do, he had come disguised.

Catherine looked around at the other ladies, a few of them had noticed him and kept their eyes downcast.

Lady Anne and her companions had not paid him any attention. Catherine feared what would happen if she was not warned, but she couldn't spoil the King's game either.

Since she was standing to the back of the crowd, she would have to push to get Lady Anne's attention covertly. Moving quickly, she tried to do just that, but, before she could say a single word, the King had reached them. And she had been able to do no more than squeeze Lady Anne's hand.

She had turned at the action and was face to face with what seemed to her a poor old man.

"Yes?" She stared at him with annoyance. Perhaps she thought this man was a messenger; he was certainly not dressed like a nobleman.

"Lady Anne, you are beautiful." The King in disguise grunted and pulled her to him, giving her a kiss.

As any woman would do when they were met with such rude behavior, she pulled away from him as fast as she could escape his grasp and slapped him across the face.

"Ser! Y-you cannot."

There was a stunned silence. Catherine went white and took a step back. Lady Anne must have looked around and seen everyone's horrified faces. No one leapt to escort this man away, and she realized something was amiss.

The King turned on his heel and strode away as fast as he could.

Lady Anne looked to her translator for an explanation. Catherine leaned forward and whispered in the translator's ear that the man who kissed her had been the King in disguise. Catherine was close enough to see Lady Anne's eyes widen, but she looked down to hide her shock and embarrassment.

Not even a moment later, the King strode in the room, this time wearing all his finery. As he stepped towards her, Lady Anne curtseyed low and stayed down until the King urged her to stand up.

"I couldn't wait to meet my future wife."

Despite his words, he looked so displeased that everyone in the room cringed.

"I-I am sorry I did not recognize you." Lady Anne's voice was a whisper.

"I don't know what you mean."

It seemed that King Henry was keen on pretending nothing had happened. Taking her cue from him, Lady Anne changed tactics.

"And you are well?"

"Indeed." Another awkward pause as he looked her over. "I shall return to Greenwich for our formal introduction."

He turned yet again and this time his companions followed him out. From behind the closed door they could hear him bellow for a horse.

Catherine saw Lady Anne grab her translator's hand, thinking no one was looking. Then she spoke quickly to her and the woman turned to Catherine.

"Is he very much displeased?"

Catherine couldn't lie. "Yes."

Lady Anne let out a heavy sigh.

Chapter Seven

There wasn't much time to dwell on what had happened. Everyone pitied Lady Anne. Though they all pretended that the King was still a handsome man, even the most delusional courtier knew that he had grown fat and stank in his old age.

There was a bear baiting and a tableaux by a professional troupe of actors. It was supposed to depict her upcoming wedding. A beautiful lady journeyed by sea to be united with her handsome lover. Bringing prosperity to his nation. The play seemed to have a biting irony that even the Lady Anne couldn't miss.

But it was not Catherine who was by her side throughout the day but Jane Boleyn. The woman was spineless in her maneuvering. She was all sweetness and comfort, saying that the King would forget and they would be happy.

Catherine wasn't so stupid as to believe her, knowing the King never forgot an insult, but Anne of Cleves was new to court and she wanted to believe that her marriage would go ahead without any impediments.

The next day they began their travels towards Blackheath.

Lady Anne was escorted by the Dukes of Norfolk and Suffolk.

Catherine had avoided her uncle's gaze when he entered the solar to greet the lady. She was sure he would have an audience with her. After all, she was here to collect information for the family as well.

She saw he must have been warned that the King was unhappy with her, for he had greeted Lady Anne coolly and spoke more to the Duke of Suffolk rather than to her or any of the other German lords and advisors. To the trained eye, this would have been seen as a snub, but the Germans did not know much about the customs in England and were too busy taking in the sights to pay attention.

The language barrier didn't help much either.

Kitty Howard had become popular overnight from her brilliant imitation of the future Queen. She had her down perfectly. Catherine thought this was particularly cruel of her, as Lady Anne had been nothing but civil to all of them.

As their journey came to an end, they could see the tops of tents with banners fluttering in the wind. All over the field, pavilions had been set up and tents pitched with rich cloth. In the center was a tent made from cloth of gold and all the German lords had exclaimed at the richness of it.

It sparkled and shone in the sunlight.

Of course, this was nothing in comparison to the sights at the Field of Cloth of gold. Where a whole makeshift castle was set up and cloth of gold was hanging everywhere, with wine flowing from fountains.

Along the way, the crowd of Londoners had come to greet their new Queen as the people had done in Calais. Of course, these were a selected few personages. Like the Mayor of London, aldermen, merchants and guild leaders. Many of the lords and ladies were already in her train.

Then the King appeared mounted on a great charger. He approached their party, on either side of him were his yeomen of the guards and his chosen companions behind him. Catherine could see Cromwell, as he stood out among the gold and blazing colors with his black cloak.

Henry was ablaze of jewels and gold in his handsome suit which included a purple velvet coat embroidered with gold damask and lace. Peaking through the slits of the coat was his shirt made of cloth of gold. Around his neck hung a collar of large diamonds and white pearls. Around his waist, his girdle and sword hilt were studded with emeralds and other precious jewels. Even his cap was decorated with jewels.

To Catherine, he looked more gaudy than magnificent, but she would never let her opinions show.

His outfit certainly impressed the Germans who stared in amazement at him.

As he was helped down from his horse, so was Lady Anne, and she was led to the top of the pavilion where two chairs were set up, Henry's higher and covered in expensive cloth. She curtseyed to him and he kissed her hand to the applause of the people gathered to watch them.

Catherine, who had been holding her breath, was amazed by how amiable the King seemed to be today. He was in a much better mood and was joking and laughing to those around him.

Musicians played a piece he had composed for the event and a lad recited a poem.

The London Mayor came forth with a gift from the people of London to Lady Anne. It was a fine roll of purple damask silk. The color of royalty — only members of the royal family were permitted to wear the color.

Then the King snapped his fingers, and two page boys came forth carrying a large box. He motioned for Lady Anne to open it, and she gasped in amazement when she found beautiful sables inside. The crowd clapped when the boys turned to show them to everyone.

"Thank you!" she exclaimed. The King nodded as though they weren't an extravagant gift.

Catherine saw Kitty twitch at the sight of them. The girl could be as jealous as a five-year-old.

After a few more professions of loyalty and prayers by the Bishops and other important personages, they were escorted to the Palace at Greenwich.

Catherine did not retire with the ladies but rather held back, sipping some spiced wine by the window sill, watching Lady Lisle and Lady Brown converse by the fire. There was no one around, and, though they glanced Catherine's way, they thought she wasn't paying attention.

"My husband says the King swore he would not marry her."

"Really?" Lady Brown was horrified. "But he cannot back out now."

"Exactly, that's the problem, isn't it? Cromwell is said to be sleepless with anxiety over this."

"There can't be an impediment to the match? They spent half a year going over the documents."

There was a soft knock at the door, and a man in Howard livery entered.

"I am to deliver a message to Lady Carey and Lady Rochford."

Catherine stepped down from her seat. "Lady Rochford is

asleep but I am Lady Carey, her niece. I will see that she gets the message."

He looked skeptical for a moment, but then nodded and handed her the letters. Catherine broke the seal on her letter. The message was a simple instruction to come see her uncle when she got the chance. She pocketed Jane's letter without opening it. Likely, it said the same thing.

"My uncle wishes to see me," she explained to the curious ladies behind her.

"I can come now if you will escort me," she said to the messenger.

"Of course," he bowed.

Her uncle was at his desk, going over papers. He had not yet retired for the night and welcomed her in.

"I am surprised to see you are the first to jump to my summons."

"Jane was asleep," she said. She stood before him, as he had not invited her to sit.

"So what can you tell me about Anne of Cleves?"

"She is pleasant and seems to be very kind."

Her uncle waved away. "No, girl. I don't need to hear you flattering her. I am sure you have heard by now the King is not happy with the match."

Catherine nodded, she played with the chain around her waist.

"So..."

She wasn't sure what he wanted her to say, but she told him all she knew.

"It was that first meeting. She slapped him when he was in disguise, and I think he was furious with her. Perhaps he still is." Her uncle nodded. Everyone had heard about this event. "She doesn't know about our English customs and is unwilling to wear some of the English gowns we offered to her."

"Why not?"

"She says they are too revealing."

He laughed. "Go on."

"Of course, she goes to mass like the rest of us, but I can tell she is uncomfortable."

"Oh?" His interest was piqued. "Have you seen her praying in German or reading any prohibited books?"

"Not as far as I know, My Lord." Catherine took a step back. "She is just confused. She doesn't know Latin and barely any English. I am sure with time she will come to learn and understand."

"You know, if she was to show any heretical tendencies, the marriage could be called off."

"But she is allowed to practice her religion. The King knew she was a Protestant." Catherine earned a glare for her outspokenness.

"Only in private. So if you or anyone has seen her acting otherwise then we have grounds to complain," he snapped.

"I see. I am sorry." Catherine's eyes were downcast.

"The King only wishes to find a good Queen for the country. You understand that. We have to make sure she is fit," he said. His tone was now softer and more placating. "You've done well, though. If you continue being helpful to me, you shall be rewarded. Keep an eye out and report to me anything you think of vital importance. I shall summon you occasionally to hear your reports."

"Yes, thank you, my lord." Catherine curtseyed and left the room.

She didn't need an escort, knowing the way back to the Queen's apartments. Along the way she passed by the great hall where she spotted a familiar figure playing cards. It made her stop in her tracks. There was Francis, laughing jovially with some other young gentlemen.

He must have sensed someone looking at him because, much to her embarrassment, he looked up and noticed her in the doorway. He gave her a little wave; she gave him a quick wary smile before strolling away.

Her mind was not on Francis but rather on what her uncle had said and what he wanted from her. She wasn't sure she could do what he was implying nor was she sure she wanted to.

To betray someone she was serving seemed like a grave sin.

In the morning, she handed Jane Boleyn the letter, watching as she checked the seal and was surprised to find it unopened.

"I wouldn't read sealed letters," Catherine said.

"But many would," Jane replied.

They were among the first to enter Anne's rooms and found her dressing with her translator.

"No, my lady. You have us to dress you." Jane rushed forward to explain. "And you shouldn't be helping someone else dress either."

Catherine moved to take over tying up the translator's sleeves to the bodice of her dress, with a hapless smile.

Anne was a bit confused once she grasped Jane's meaning but she shrugged. "I am no Queen yet. Mistress Loew is my lady, nothing strange in Cleves."

"Alright, but not after your wedding." Jane clicked her tongue in disapproval at the gown.

"You are sure you don't want something else?" Motioning

to her dress which made her slim figure appear fat and ungainly.

"Perhaps not this." Anne put aside the high-necked undershirt.

It was an improvement at least.

With Anne dressed and wearing her heavy German head-dress, they went into her privy chamber to sit until the King came to escort them to mass. Catherine found it strange he chose not to break his fast with his betrothed. In fact, he seemed perfectly content to never see her again.

Anne was, as usual, ignorant to this, but the rest of the court was buzzing with how ill-suited she was to the King.

They had an evening of dancing and entertainment and the next day the journey to Westminster was supposed to take place for the wedding. This plan was put aside for another day as the King claimed the weather was not suited for travel and his leg was giving him pain.

Even Anne was skeptical of this but did not complain, as she had seen him attempt a dance with Kitty Howard, who had managed to push herself to the forefront of the ladies.

Anne's translator approached her with an uneasy expression.

"There is no trouble?" she asked in her ear.

Catherine shrugged. "It's the weather," she said slowly. "Foul tempered winds."

She paused over every word and the translator seemed to grasp what she was hinting at. It wasn't the weather that was in a foul mood but the King.

"She was shocked by the kiss." She tried to explain, but Catherine, who thought she had implicated herself enough of this, stepped away with a smile.

"I hope all will be well in the future."

The translator seemed to understand that she was

treading on dangerous ground. "You've been more helpful than anyone else." She thanked Catherine.

Catherine had surprised herself by giving away so much. All the other ladies had seemed so tight-lipped.

In a sense of irony, it appeared as though Jane Boleyn and Kitty Howard had become Anne's favorites. Both these women were after their own gains, but they could be charming and entertaining enough to fool anyone into thinking they were good friends.

Kitty, who was now sporting a gold pendant given to her by the King, was on the lookout for more rewards. Besides the King, Anne was already proving to be generous. She let Kitty borrow some pearls when the young girl had mentioned that she didn't have a single thing to wear to dinner.

Catherine tried not to be envious. She was not playing the same games as the other ladies. She wanted to be helpful, not use Anne.

Finally, when it was obvious to the King that he could not find a concrete reason to put off the wedding without insulting Cleves and the Protestant League, he declared that the wedding could proceed. Although, not before embarrassing his fiancé by demanding she swear before the council that she was free to marry and was not pre-contracted to wed someone else.

Grand barges had been brought to escort everyone from Greenwich to Westminster. Their party made a spectacular entrance — crowds of commoners had watched from the shore and waved as the barges decked in precious cloth went past them.

The King was all smiles, standing proudly at the helm of

his own barge under the canopy of estate. At his side, dressed in a beautiful cream gown, was Anne, who waved with a warm smile to the people.

They had a private ceremony inside Westminster, and, as one of her maids of honor, Catherine watched from the back of the chapel as the couple said their vows before the Archbishop. Her motto would be 'God send me well to keep'.

Catherine couldn't help thinking that here was another motto for yet another Queen.

Having emerged from the chapel, the King led his new Queen to the dining hall for feasting and dancing. For the time being, Catherine would be released from her duties and left to her own devices.

The ladies dispersed from their table as soon as the platters of food had finished coming around. They took up dancing partners or went to speak to other friends or family. Catherine was alone at the table, happy to be sitting after the long travels the previous days.

A tap on her shoulder made her turn to look behind her. A strange young man was there.

"Pardon my forwardness, Katherine Howard suggested you might like to dance?"

Catherine was going to object but could think of no reason not to say yes.

"My cousin is quite outspoken. But I shall dance with you. What is your name?"

"Richard Grey." He gave her a little bow.

She stood and let him lead her to the dance floor, already packed with partners.

"Perhaps you can ask your cousin to dance with me when she is next free?"

Catherine wasn't surprised by the question. "Mister Grey,

I shall try because you look hopelessly in love with her." She laughed when he shook his head.

"No, I have no eyes for any but you." He twirled her round.

"You cannot lie to me." Catherine had seen him trying to catch Kitty's eyes even as he tried to make conversation with her.

"Don't think I am insulted." She reassured him, seeing him blush.

Once the dance ended, she led him over to Kitty. "Katherine, you must do me the favor and let Richard Grey have the next dance with you."

Kitty looked him up and down, giving him one of her toothy grins. "I have so many men asking me to dance."

"But he is graceful and just the right height for you," Catherine said.

"Alright then. I shall dance with you, Master Grey. I am afraid you shall be the envy of all of these other men though." Indeed the group of men around her seemed displeased.

Catherine left them to fight over her and tried to weave her way back to her seat when someone stopped her.

"I was hoping to run into you, Lady Carey." It was Francis Knollys again.

"Good evening, Master Knollys." She met his gaze head on.

"Would you care to dance?"

Catherine, who was feeling tired, hesitated, her feet were aching.

"Perhaps you would prefer someone else?" He looked over to Richard Grey, who was dancing with Kitty.

She shook her head. "Not at all, I am simply tired. But I shall accept your offer as thanks for your help on the boat."

He doffed his cap to her. "Then I shall accept the wonderful reward."

They took their places in line as a galliard began. She asked him questions as the dance began with them taking slow steps beside each other.

"And where are you from?"

"My family home is in Berkshire, but my mother resides in a home near Essex."

"That's where my family is." Catherine was surprised. "I never heard of a Knollys neighbor."

"My father and I mostly lived at court, and my mother was never one to entertain. My father was a companion to the King's late father and then served King Henry until his death."

"And you are following in his footsteps?"

"As best as I can."

"Do you like being at court?"

"As all good courtiers must." He smiled.

The dance began in earnest now and they had to take turns making their jumps. She admired the way he made them seem so effortless.

"And are you happy here?"

"Yes." Catherine wasn't lying entirely.

They spoke of trifles whenever the dance allowed them to talk, and then he walked her back to her seat.

"I shall leave you to rest now, Lady Carey."

Catherine tried to remain indifferent as she watched him go. Everyone flirted and danced with ladies of the court. There was nothing special about him asking for a dance. Besides, he probably thought she was besotted with him from the way she had stopped to look at him back at Greenwich. She had only stopped because it had surprised her to have recognized someone at last.

Many of the faces she saw at court were still new, and he made her feel at ease. As she promised herself to put thoughts of him aside, the King stood up.

It was time for the bedding ceremony.

Catherine was not among those chosen to be witness to it. But she went alongside the other ladies in waiting to prepare Anne for bed. She helped undress her mistress and pack away her rich gown. Others helped her into her nightgown and plaited her hair. Then they led her into the chamber.

Catherine did not follow. Instead, she went to bed saying a silent prayer for Anne.

The next day, the ladies knocked on the Queen's door.

"Come in," she called.

The ladies came in with sheepish eyes, but they were surprised to find the bed barely slept in. The King had left at some point during the night, and Anne looked as if she hadn't been touched. Her hair was still neatly plaited. There were none of the tell-tale signs that the wedding was consummated.

"Are you ready to get up, your grace?" Jane was already by her side, but Catherine could see she was just trying to be the first to get a look at the sheets to confirm everyone's suspicions.

"Yes."

They helped her wash and dress and then proceeded to mass as would be the habit every day.

Now Queen Anne looked serene during the ceremony. She was likely warned to conform to the English way of worship or else she would displease the King.

No one else's thoughts were on prayer that morning, though. They all wondered what had taken place the night before. Everyone thought of the King — perhaps he had been struck with impotence. After all, the pain in his leg was hurting him so badly.

Before noon, the news was spread around the palace that the King found his new wife so distasteful that he could not do the deed. He had claimed out loud that he did not think she was a virgin at all. No one informed Queen Anne about this. For once, Catherine had to agree that blissful ignorance was preferred in this case.

That very same day, the Flemish lords who had accompanied her departed for home. Now the new Queen was left with only Mistress Loew and the ambassador Karl Harst for companions.

As she settled down to begin her royal marriage, the machinations of the court began stirring. With the King so displeased and already wanting to escape his wife many sensed an opportunity to rise to power.

Chapter Eight

Everyone seemed to pick the same enemy: Thomas Cromwell. Simply, by being the King's favorite, he had made himself unpopular. His policies against the churches and monasteries had made the King rich but filled the people's hearts with fury. He was seen as the enemy of England, and now he was left weak. He had been the one to suggest the Cleves marriage, and, more than that, he had pushed it forward.

But nothing was done in the open. Cromwell could still be dangerous, and the King's foul mood could turn yet again. So day by day, courtiers slowly dropped a word in the King's ear whenever they could. Or made a complaint.

"Master Cromwell knew about the Queen's unsuitability."

"Cromwell thinks to rule in your place."

"Cromwell is pushing forward heretical policies."

Catherine heard whispers such as these all day long.

With the court separated into those who supported the marriage and those who were against it, Anne was unable to make any headway with her husband.

Henry visited her bed several times a week, but, still,

Catherine and the other ladies found her untouched in the morning. With every day that passed, it seemed that the King found her more and more distasteful. He avoided her rooms and rarely spoke to her while they dined together. He even refused to admit her Flemish ambassador, claiming he was too busy. Catherine often spotted Karl Harst hunkered down on a seat at the back of the dining hall each evening, eating as if he had not eaten all day. It was likely he had not.

It was no secret that the King refused to pay him any wages for his work, and, likewise, his master, the Duke of Cleves, refused to do the same. The Duke felt it was the responsibility of his sister to pay for his upkeep, but, since she was given no money of her own, she could not oblige her brother.

Catherine and all the ladies had been witness to the letters she received from home berating her for her failing to help Cleves. Often Anne would shed a tear and look imploringly at Mrs. Loew for help. How could she make her brother understand that, though the King gave her dresses and jewels to wear, he had not given her any money nor had he even made plans to have her crowned yet?

The one thing the whole court was concerned about was the fact that the King seemed unable to consummate his marriage. Everyone wished to see another son born to the King to secure the line of succession and maintain peace in the realm.

Strangely, Anne was the only one who acted as if there was nothing wrong with her marriage. It prompted Lady Rutland to speak with her one evening as the ladies sat together working on shirts for the King.

"Your grace, is all well between you and his majesty?"

"Oh, he is very kind," Anne assured her. Her English was improving, though it seemed that the accent was here to stay.

"But at night? — When you are alone? — Do you not want children?" Lady Rutland was driven to speak more plainly by her innocence.

"Very kind. When he comes to bed he kisses me, and he takes me by the hand, and bids me 'Good night, sweetheart'; and in the morning, kisses me and bids me 'Farewell, darling'. I pray to God that I shall have a child soon."

All the ladies balked.

"Your grace, there must be more than this, or we will never have a Duke of York, which this realm desires so much."

"I shall pray."

Jane Boleyn spoke to stop Lady Rutland speaking further. "We shall all pray, too."

"Amen." The women gave each other a knowing look. Her innocence was a disaster whether she was pretending at it or not. But either for decorum's sake or due to political alliances, no one else spoke, and they turned back to working on embroidery.

With Lent upon them, some of the ladies from the Queen's chamber were invited to take part in a masque. Catherine was honored to be among those chosen. The court would soon abstain from any frivolity, so this would be her last chance to enjoy herself as she tended to not go on hunts. Her horsemanship skills weren't up to par, and she found being in the saddle uncomfortable.

They practiced with the Master of Revels directing them around. While the fool was just as busy distracting them with tricks and juggling.

The masque would be titled Blooming Roses — about

young loves encountering each other for the first time, only for the sin of jealousy to come between them and try to separate them. A model garden was being built and the girls would emerge from behind rose bushes, in brightly colored dresses, then the men would enter and they would perform a dance. At the sound of the drum, a man in black would appear and steal the girls away from each man in succession as they tried to escape him. It would conclude with a knight appearing and slaying the man, picking from the girls a favorite to crown the loveliest.

So far they hadn't been able to get through the ladies emerging without giggles and interruptions. Mistress Loew, whose task had been to oversee the maids in waiting and ensure proper decorum was maintained, was kept busy reprimanding them when some like Kitty became too forward with the gentlemen.

"Master Farlyton, perhaps the girls should practice without the men?" she suggested, and he was inclined to agree with her.

"A pity," a familiar voice said. Catherine looked to her side and saw that Francis was beside her now.

"How come?"

"I just traded Culpeper for his place, but now I won't be able to dance with you." That meant he would be her partner for the masque.

"That's a shame," she said, trying not to look flattered by the fact he kept going out of his way to be with her.

He disappeared with the rest of the men, and she had to concentrate now on dancing. Later that day, she asked Anne Basset what she knew of him.

"Is he... married?" Catherine wasn't sure how to word the question.

"Not that I am aware. He is the King's companion and

among his favorites, but I've never seen him with a woman or heard any gossip about him." Anne gave her a knowing smile. "Has he caught your eye? He is not that bad looking, but he doesn't have many credentials to recommend him. You could do better."

By that, she meant he was not rich. Catherine shrugged.

"I was merely curious. I would never do anything without my family's permission." That was true. She had been witness to the consequences of disobedience too often. But now she knew she had no reason to hide from his smiles and company.

The Queen came out of her private rooms looking flushed, and Catherine went to her side.

"Can I help you, your grace?"

"I don't know — what is the word for frömmigkeit?"

Catherine could only shake her head at the strange German word. Anne waved Mrs. Loew over to her and asked her.

"Ah! Piety. What were you trying to say?"

Anne fiddled with one of the rings on her finger, and she explained in German. Catherine furrowed her eyebrows not able to comprehend. All she could determine of the conversation was Princess Mary.

The two women turned to her and Mrs. Loew asked her quietly, "The King is not happy with the Princess Mary because she is too pious?"

"No, only because she follows the old way. Her mother's religion," Catherine said.

"He will not allow her to court because of this?"

Catherine struggled with how to answer the blunt question. It was more complicated than that. The Princess had fought with her father for years and refused to recognize the new church or his marriage to Anne Boleyn. It was no secret that she remained a staunch Catholic, though she had managed to reconcile with her father after signing a document submitting herself to his authority.

"She has argued with him." Catherine decided to impart this knowledge to them, for she had heard it spoken about in the halls. "He wants to betroth her to the Duke of Bavaria — a Protestant." Her voice getting lower as she stressed the word Protestant.

Mrs. Loew translated and Catherine saw a look of understanding cross Anne's face.

"Would not be a good match," she said in her stilted English.

"The King knows best." Catherine would never say anything to incriminate herself.

Anne smiled knowingly. "Thank you, Lady Carey. You are very good."

Catherine bobbed a small curtsey and retreated.

Later, she found Mistress Loew and took a seat beside her at the table.

"Can I help you?"

"Would you teach me some German?" Catherine kept her tone sweet and innocent.

Mistress Loew was still skeptical. "Why?"

"To help the Queen, and I love to learn." Catherine didn't break eye contact with the stern woman.

"I shall teach you a little. You are a good girl, not like the others."

Catherine knew she was referring to Kitty and Anne Basset, whose talents for flirting and dancing were well known.

It was agreed that she would sit with her before bed going over some German words and phrases. Catherine knew that with this she would be able to understand the Queen better as well — her uncle's instructions were at the back of her mind. She was to find out everything she could.

If the Queen wrote messages in German, perhaps she would be able to know what they said.

———

The day of Shrovetide was upon the court before they knew it. During the day, they walked to the lists and watched the men joust and hold mock duels before the cheering crowd. Then, before dinner was the masque.

Catherine was dressed in a light gown of orange organza — the ladies around her, including Kitty Howard and Anne Basset, wore similar gowns in different colors. They looked like flowers indeed. They wore their hair loose with crowns of silk flowers on their heads. She spied Francis dressed in a suit of the same shade of orange as her dress. He caught her eye and gave her a wink.

They took their place before the Queen and the waiting court on the elaborate stage. The Master of Revels announced the start of the masque and off they went dancing through their steps.

At the end, there was applause, and the white knight, who remained masked, was given a wreath of flowers to award to the loveliest girl. He stopped before Kitty Howard, who curtseyed very low and thanked him *oh so very much*. Catherine saw how she leaned herself forward to give the knight a good view of her breasts.

As instructed, the girls asked in unison for the brave knight to reveal himself, though they all knew who it was already. They applauded as the King showed his face, his cheeks beet red from exertion.

He returned to his seat beside the Queen, but Catherine

saw how he looked after Kitty hungrily. There was a time when she had thought he preferred Anne Basset, but Kitty had managed to win his attention.

The Princess Mary had attended the day's celebrations, but she looked pale and her inattention to what was going on around her made Catherine suspect that she was very much concerned with the potential betrothal with the Duke of Bavaria.

Her uncle caught her attention and motioned with the crook of his finger for her to join him at his table. Catherine made her way over as inconspicuously as possible. She curtseyed before the great Duke, and he greeted her with a smile.

"Court life suits you, niece."

She nodded, waiting for him to get to the point.

"Are things the same in the Queen's rooms?" His voice was so low she could barely hear him.

"Yes."

"The Princess Mary has spoken to her of the Duke of Bavaria?"

"She knows of it and that the Princess does not wish to marry him."

"She does not?" He pinpointed that, and, from his smile, she knew he thought he had caught the Princess in disobeying her father.

"What I meant to say is that the Princess Mary has reservations about the match. I doubt she would ever disobey the King."

"Has the Queen said anything to the King?"

Catherine shrugged. "I don't think so."

"Perhaps she should be encouraged to do so."

"But..."

He turned his pointed gaze to her now, fully giving her his attention. She bowed her head apologetically.

"Perhaps she can stop the engagement. It would suit our purposes either way."

At Catherine's inquisitive gaze, he graced her with an explanation. "I am traveling to France to meet with the King and discuss a possible treaty. An alliance with a Protestant Duke would not look good. And any further trouble between the newlyweds would be helpful too."

It was no secret that her uncle held to the Catholic faith in his heart, though he prayed according to the King's wishes

"I'll do what I can."

"Good." He waved her away.

Catherine walked away with a heavy heart. She struggled with what she was instructed to do. It sounded too dangerous, and she had just gained a foothold with Mrs. Loew. There was no reason for her to betray the Queen by giving her bad advice.

The next day she realized she needn't have bothered with keeping her own mouth shut, for Lady Rochford was by Anne's side, ready with the suggestion that she should talk to the King about Princess Mary.

"I shall see." Anne's response was hesitant and noncommittal. Catherine hid a smile by searching through the box for another color of thread. The Queen was smarter than she looked. Even in the short time since she had met him, she knew that Henry did not like to be crossed.

Anne had been shocked to see the easy way the court kept Lent. There was no red meat but plenty of chicken and other pheasant. The food was just as rich and bountiful as ever before. She refused to touch many of the dishes and sipped at broth and bread.

"How did you keep Lent in Cleves?" Catherine asked Mrs. Loew.

"Only fish and very plain food."

Catherine nodded. She was starting to get a better picture of the strict world of Anne's upbringing.

One day, the King announced he would visit the Queen's room in the evening, and her rooms were in chaos as her servants set about tidying up and arranging for extra tables and chairs to be brought in. The ladies changed their gowns, and then they all waited patiently for his arrival.

As he entered, everyone curtseyed low. Catherine's attention was on the men who had joined him. To her disappointment, it did not seem Francis was among them.

The King kissed Anne's hand, and she flushed at the contact but had the good sense to smile at him and not pull away.

"Would you like to play cards?" she asked him.

They sat down at a table and began a game of cent. She won but had the good graces to call for another game, and, this time, Catherine, who stood behind her, watched her make poor decisions in order to let her husband win.

"You must teach me to play, your majesty." His chest puffed out at the compliment, and for once he smiled at her.

"I am the best after all."

They spoke amicably before the rest of the ladies and courtiers. Then he asked her if she would like to accompany him for a glass of wine in one of her more private rooms. Of course, they wouldn't be fully alone. Mistress Loew motioned for Catherine to follow them in, holding the goblets on a silver tray while a manservant carried in the jug of wine.

She stood with her back pressed against the wall, ready to serve but listening to every word and watching every gesture.

"You have befriended the Princess Mary." The statement almost seemed like an accusation.

"Yes, I hope that pleases you."

"I am surprised she would be so friendly to you."

Anne seemed to gulp back a comment at the insult.

"Well, I have been negotiating an engagement between her and the Duke of Bavaria. Perhaps you can speak to her to prepare herself for marriage. I know it has been put off for far too long."

Catherine could sense the challenge in his voice but Anne seemed unconcerned.

"Perhaps Princess Mary would like someone else? The Dukedom of Bavaria very far from England."

The King's grip on his goblet tightened.

"What are you saying, Madam?"

Anne met his fury head on. "She would not be happy."

"Her happiness is in serving me and the country."

"Yes, of course. But perhaps another prince would be better." Anne still did not look away.

Now Catherine's eyes remained focused on a spot on the floor, ready for one of the King's rages.

"They told me you were docile, Madam, but I see that, among the other lies, you are not." He gulped down his wine.

"I only am looking for the best." Anne was stumbling over her words now.

"And you still can't speak English." The King was laughing at her now.

Anne disregarded his cruelty. "I am learning."

The King threw the goblet and Catherine watched the precious metal bounce on the floor and roll into a corner. This was not the first time she had seen him rage, and she pressed herself against the wall, the panels digging into her back.

"Not fast enough, it seems."

The King limped towards the door and threw it open. To the courtiers outside, he pretended he was in a good mood, calling for Anne Basset to play him a song.

The Queen had not moved, but, knowing they would talk if she did not reappear, she straightened her gown, smoothing her hands over the embroidered petticoat.

"Some more wine, your grace?" Catherine asked.

"No." Anne shook her head. "No need."

Catherine followed her out of the room.

That evening, just as she was ready to get to bed, Jane Boleyn popped her head in the room.

"Catherine, we are summoned to see the Duke. Put on a robe and let's go."

Catherine shook her head. "I cannot."

"Catherine Carey, do you wish to be dismissed from court?"

At the threat, Catherine pulled on a thick robe and threw on her hood to maintain some modesty.

She followed after Jane, not through the usual main passage ways but rather secret back doors and galleries. Jane nudged her to enter the door, and she followed closely behind.

The Duke of Norfolk was standing by the window. If she didn't know him better, she would have thought that he was looking forlorn.

"Your grace." The two women bowed in greeting.

"Ah, my little assistants. What news do you have for me?"

Jane nudged Catherine to speak, but she wasn't sure what he wanted to hear.

"Come along — I know you were witness to the King's conversation with the Queen tonight."

Word seemed to have gotten around quickly. Catherine threw a glance at Lady Rochford, who seemed fascinated with her nails.

"He took her aside to talk."

"The King was confiding in her?" Her uncle gave a bark like laugh.

"He was enjoying her company but then she displeased him." Catherine refused to go into details. She knew now that he wasn't merely keeping abreast of the news in the court. He had something far more sinister in mind.

"And how did she manage that?"

Catherine had a choice to be loyal to her family or her Queen. She tried for a middle road.

"She always manages that. The King is usually irked by her mere presence." It hurt Catherine to disrespect Queen Anne, who was such a kind and trusting mistress. She never spoke harshly to anyone and was always quick to help in any way she could.

Her uncle and Lady Rochford were trained courtiers and were not fooled by her though.

"I think you should wrack that brain of yours for a better answer. Remember who you owe the very clothes on your back to!" Her uncle was hardly trying to hide his displeasure as he took a step towards her. "If I had not convinced your father to take your mother back under his good graces instead of disinheriting her, you and her brood would be living in a hovel on a farm somewhere scrounging for food. If I had not found you this place at court you would be forgotten in the country. So?"

"She told the King that the Princess Mary wouldn't be happy with the Duke of Bavaria." The words came spilling out as she trembled in her fear.

"Ah, so she dared to speak out — I didn't think she would have it in her," Lady Rochford said, her arms crossed in front of her.

The Duke patted Catherine on the head as though she was a pet dog. She fought her instincts to step away from him.

"You have done well to serve your family. I shall see you are rewarded as long as you learn to understand now who to give your loyalty to."

"Yes, my lord." Catherine bobbed a polite curtsey. With her downcast eyes, she appeared to be the very representation of female servility, and the Duke turned away from her to ask Jane questions now.

However, Catherine was far from reprimanded. Inside she was plotting her escape. She did not wish to be a part of his games. Anne did not deserve it.

"I hear that the Queen is trying to get Master Cromwell to meet with her. If he does, make sure one of you are present and report to me everything that is being said."

"Catherine you may leave." The Duke waved her away and invited Lady Rochford to take a seat. "Bennett will escort you back to your rooms." He had called for his manservant, who appeared like a silent shadow.

They were done with her but she wasn't done with them. Catherine and her escort were nearly back to the Queen's apartments when Catherine pretended to have remembered something.

"OH! I forgot my rosary in the chapel."

The man glared.

"I must get it or Mistress Loew will be upset with me in

the morning. I am so careless." Catherine looked positively frightened. "I can go by myself. I know the way."

The man was now frowning and he seemed tempted.

"You've almost taken me back. I shall be fine from here. There's no way I would get lost, and I won't tell my uncle. You must be tired." She gave him a piteous look.

"Alright, lady. But you promise you won't give me any trouble later?"

"I promise." This wasn't really a lie. Catherine turned to walk towards the chapel, but, once she saw that Bennett had disappeared back to her uncle's room, she followed after him.

There was no one guarding the front door to his rooms, but would she dare sneak in? The door would surely squeak and alert them even from the inner chamber. She glanced around and saw no one was around. She even pressed her ear to the door trying to make out if anyone was inside.

Finally, she took the risk and tried the door.

It opened a crack and she got a good view of the empty receiving room. The only light came from the moonlight outside, leaving the room in darkness. It was late and the servants were asleep. She could always have an excuse ready if she was discovered. So she slipped inside the robe she was wearing, making her smaller and easier to maneuver around the furniture. She kept to the wall, ready to hide behind a bookcase if someone appeared.

She reached the door to her uncle's office where he was sequestered with the Lady Rochford and listened through the keyhole.

"And the King seems to continue to favor her?"

"Certainly," Jane Boleyn answered. "He doesn't keep this a secret."

"But he hasn't managed to do anything with her?"

"She has kissed him."

"It can go no further." Catherine could feel the Duke's anger. "The little slut has to act the part of an innocent girl. Can she not manage that?"

"I will speak to her."

"Is she such a fool that she does not realize how much she could stand to gain if she just plays this correctly?"

"I shall put the idea in her head. Leave it to me, my lord. All she wants are more jewels and gowns. She loves attention and is easily persuaded."

"Good, she can have those if she does as we say, but I will not have another Anne. A chance like this won't come again."

"Do you think the King will put the Queen aside?"

"Certainly, Gardiner is already looking for evidence. The French are no longer allied with the Spanish so now we no longer need the Cleves alliance."

"So quickly?"

"Why not? But it will go quicker if the King falls in love again, and it would be best if he falls in love with a Howard girl."

Catherine pulled away from the door. She thought she could hear footsteps coming from the antechamber and rushed back out the door of her uncle's apartments. Her heart was pounding as she made her way back to her own rooms, praying she wouldn't stumble into anyone.

So that's what her uncle was after. Putting a girl like Kitty Howard in the way of the King. She would never have thought of it herself. After all, Kitty was such a flirt and loose with her favors. She was half in love with all the handsome young men of the court already, but Catherine doubted she felt anything for the King.

Of course, she danced for him and batted her eyelashes at him, but she was after small rewards and trinkets. She was hardly lusting after him. However, Catherine knew how easily convinced she could be. It wouldn't take much for her to realize the benefit of being in the King's good graces.

There was nothing she could do openly, but she would wait and bide her time. Keeping this information to herself until she could see what she could do with it. Should she warn Anne of what was being planned? No. Besides what could Anne do? She only had Karl Harst to help her and he was little more than useless.

Kitty giggled when she saw Catherine sneak into their shared room. "And where have you been?"

"None of your business, Kitty."

"Fine I won't tell you where I have been either."

"You've been somewhere?" Catherine furrowed her eyebrows.

"I met with Thomas Culpeper. He asked me to see him in the gardens." She was not ashamed to share this information with anyone.

Catherine blushed at the implications. "But your honor. Kitty, if anyone finds out..."

"We didn't do anything! Well, he kissed me and gave me a rose." She held it up to her. "He's so handsome."

"And you? Were you with that Francis you have your eye on?"

"Of course not!" Catherine crossed her arms indignantly in front of her. She would never dare be so brazen as to meet a man alone at night.

"Well, I highly recommend it or someone else will snatch him up."

"I never said I liked him." Catherine climbed in under the covers leaving her robe on the trunk at the foot of her bed.

"You never said you didn't." Kitty laughed. "Did you know Thomas said he would ask to carry my favor at the next joust?

Of course, he's not the first to ask me, but I think I shall say yes to him and to Edmund."

Catherine ignored her but this didn't stop Kitty from prattling on and on about the wonderful Thomas.

In the morning, Jane had positioned herself at Kitty's side, whispering in her ear for the entire mass. Catherine knew what Jane must be telling her poor relation. Kitty's eyes were wide and her mouth parted open as if she had been surprised as they walked back to the Queen's rooms.

Catherine asked her if she had seen Culpeper trying to get her attention when the King had bid the Queen good morning.

"He did? I did not see." Clearly her mind was elsewhere, for she had been gushing over him just the night before. Then her eyes looked up in surprise at Catherine. "He really shouldn't be. There's no reason he should be making eyes at me. He means nothing to me."

Catherine was taken aback.

"I am an honorable girl, and I don't think about boys." Kitty walked faster to catch up to Anne Basset.

Catherine's eyebrow arched watching her go. How quickly she changed her tune and how quickly she lied. She thought it would be prudent to tell her uncle that his chosen one was highly unsuited for the position he was intent on pushing her towards.

Chapter Nine

Catherine waited a week before approaching her uncle. During this time, she had seen Kitty go out riding alone with the King and dance before him, her attention fixed on him. But Catherine could see how she would look over at Culpeper when she thought no one was looking.

"You wanted to see me?" The Duke raised his eyebrow, surprised by her willingness to come forward.

"You told me to come to you with any information I thought was important."

"So I did." He looked expectantly at her, satisfied that she seemed to know her place now.

"I thought you might like to know that Katherine Howard is all but in love with Thomas Culpeper." This was not a complete exaggeration.

The Duke's face was expressionless. He hid his interest in the subject well, but she saw how his fingers had tightened their grip on the arm of his chair for the briefest of moments.

"She is my cousin and I would not want a blemish on our reputation and honor." Catherine offered this as a reason for giving the information.

"She has spoken to him and seen him?"

"May I be blunt? She often sneaks out of the maid's chamber at night. She's not the only one, of course, but I think you would want to talk to her."

He fixed those hawk-like eyes of his on her, but she did not squirm under his gaze.

"And do you sneak off at night too? Or do you merely creep around in the shadows?"

"I would never." Catherine huffed.

"Good, for it might ruin your chances at a proper marriage." Catherine looked confused. "You seem so clever and knowledgeable, but, let me assure you that you are a novice at the game of courtly intrigue."

"I never..." She took a step back.

"I suppose you don't think I've noticed how you blush and laugh with that Master Knollys. Do you think he is paying attention to you because he likes you or finds you pretty?"

Catherine bit the inside of her cheek.

"You haven't kept your own feelings so carefully hidden either, my niece, but don't worry, your honor isn't at risk for you have been betrothed. Your parents are signing the contract as we speak. You have me to thank for finding you someone willing to marry a girl of such low birth and ambiguous lineage."

Catherine's fingers were digging into her palms as she fought to keep her expression passive.

"I have not acted dishonorably in any way."

"I know you have a weakness for listening at doors." Now he was smiling brightly at her. "But thank you for bringing me this news. I was not aware of how far things had gone." He was pulling at his beard thoughtfully. "It is nothing but inno-cent courtly flirtation is it not?"

"I am sure it was," Catherine said.

"Keep an eye on her for me, since Lady Jane seems to have failed in this department. I am sure this won't hurt your conscience, and perhaps you shall be more helpful with this than you are with the Queen."

Catherine curtseyed, grinding her teeth together to stop from saying something she would regret as she left her uncle's rooms.

She had been brought low today.

She was not the sharp-minded courtier she had thought herself to be. It did not even matter to her that she was to be betrothed; it hurt that Francis had seemed to know all along, and he had tried to make her feel special by his attentions. She had let him tempt her too. She was weak. She had tried to jump too high and had fallen.

Catherine excused herself from the Queen's company, saying she was not feeling well, and, indeed, the Queen declared she was looking pale and ordered her to rest in her room. She stayed unmoving on the bed until it was time for dinner. She had managed not to cry and that small victory ensured she wouldn't show up with red eyes at the dining hall.

Even though she hoped she wouldn't have to see Francis that night, he approached her as the partners were assembling for a dance. She turned on her heel and walked away from him.

The idea of marriage did not scare her. She knew that soon she would be married off to someone, but she had thought it would be a more mutual affair. That she wouldn't be made to feel like a fool.

For two days, Catherine managed to avoid Francis, but, on the third, he cornered her on her way back from the chapel.

"May I speak to you, Lady Carey?"

Catherine's temper had cooled by then and she agreed. He didn't lead her anywhere private, lest someone get the wrong idea. Instead, he led her to the window overlooking the inner courtyard. If anyone walked by they would see a couple admiring the scenery outside.

"Why have you been avoiding me?"

The question was easy enough to answer, but Catherine felt her mouth go dry. She was unable to speak from shame of admitting she had thought he might be talking to her out of love and admiration, not out of a sense of duty.

He was waiting patiently enough so Catherine was forced to speak.

"Is there a reason for you to go out of your way to speak to me?" She watched his expression change from confusion to a look of dawning understanding.

"You have been told?"

"My uncle was kind enough to let me know. Although I suppose that I didn't need to know at all until the day of the w-wedding." Her voice cracked at that word.

Francis ran a hand through his hair.

"I wanted to spend time with you without a looming cloud hanging over our heads."

"Marriage to me would be that terrible?"

"No! Listen you are upset and rightly so. I thought, perhaps, if we got to know each other slowly then we could start off on good terms which is more than many people have."

Catherine thought of the Queen and swallowed hard.

"It has started off with lies. I thought you liked me for me, not because our families have pushed us together."

Now he looked exasperated. "I wouldn't have gone out of my way to dance and speak to you if I felt it was such a struggle to be by your side."

Catherine could feel her eyes pricking with tears. She bit the inside of her cheek again to hold them back.

"You can be angry with me, but do you think you could forgive me? If you cannot, tell me, and I will break off the betrothal."

"Then I will be nothing but unwanted goods."

Her words stung him and she saw him step back.

"I am sorry. I didn't mean anyt..." He stopped midsentence as a sob finally wracked her body.

Catherine found herself biting her fist to try to keep the sobs from escaping. He stood by her side until her tears had been spent. She was sure everyone walking by had seen. Francis took out a handkerchief and handed it to her. She looked up at him and saw how he bit his lower lip as he considered what to do. His sincerity threatened to make her cry again. So she looked away and dried her eyes, though fresh tears were still escaping.

"I know my face is ugly but I am sorry it is so awful it is making you cry."

At that Catherine laughed. "No, it's not you." She blew her nose, and, to his credit, he didn't look disgusted.

"Promise?"

"Yes." She managed a weak smile for him. "I should go — I will be missed."

"Catherine, I would not marry you if you did not want to marry me."

"How can I know that so soon? But I do not hate you."

"I will accept that for now." He took her hand and placed a kiss on her tear stained palm. "I shall try to never make you cry like that again."

"Just don't lie to me." Catherine took her hand back and disappeared. She tried to compose herself as best as she could, but Mistress Loew did not miss anything and asked her if something had happened.

"Family issues," Catherine explained in broken German.

Mistress Loew smiled at her attempt and patted her arm. "Go wash your face and return when you have caught your breath."

Her uncle was soon distracted from tormenting her by the news that Cromwell would be invested as Earl of Essex by the King and given the title of Lord Great Chamberlain of England.

On a cool night in April he had railed before both Jane and Catherine.

"Why has the King chosen to reward Cromwell now?"

Jane was dumbfounded. How was she supposed to know?

Catherine was looking at the floor but she dared to reply. "Perhaps he has found a way for the King to get rid of Anne. He is always generous when he has received good news."

The Duke slammed his hand down on the table in front of him. "That man is still responsible for this mess in the first place. He should be glad he is not in the Tower!"

"Anne has argued with him over the Lady Elizabeth. She wants him to allow her to visit court." Catherine volunteered the information.

"That should make him angrier, not ready to jump to a reward."

"But my Lord, the King wouldn't get angrier if he no longer feels trapped in his marriage."

For once, he looked at her with interest as if impressed

with her thinking. "Yes, and he has done this before, handed out awards only to throw the offender in the Tower the next day."

He straightened up and re-adjusted his doublet which had become askew during his tirade.

"Good, keep an eye out. You are dismissed."

On the day of his investiture something that Cromwell himself had been surprised about, the court enjoyed a day of celebration. In the tournament arranged, his nephew joined the lists and rode well in the joust.

Catherine found it amusing that the factions of court could be seen so easily in the faces of the courtiers. Those who supported the reformation of the church were light on their feet, ready with an easy smile at their triumph today. In contrast, those who longed for a return to the Catholic faith were sullen and ready to snap at anyone who displeased them.

Queen Anne, who had yet to receive her visit from him, found herself confused. She asked Lady Rutland if she might summon Lord Cromwell to visit her, but Lady Rutland returned with a message that he was much too busy.

If Anne had been Queen Catherine of Aragon or the other Queen Anne, she would have railed and demanded him to appear, but she did not have the authority to give orders.

No Queen of Henry's would survive long with a commanding disposition.

Anne did achieve a small victory, though, and she was allowed to take the Lady Mary and her court of ladies to visit Lady Elizabeth. This was not the royal welcome at court she desired but it was a step.

Perhaps Catherine should have warned her that even

though the King gave her permission to go, she should not, since he was so displeased with the idea.

Yet, here they were on the royal barge being rowed down the Thames to Hatfield House. Elizabeth was usually attached to the Prince's household, but she had recently taken to residing in the house, finishing her education.

The party was greeted by the assembly of the household.

Catherine's eyes went straight for her cousin and, as she secretly knew, her half-sister as well. She was tall for a seven-year-old with a pale complexion, and, even from a distance, the redness of her hair could be seen from beneath her hood.

Her governess Kat Ashley stood by her side but did not hold her hand nor did she need to assist this clever child who knew how to greet the visiting Queen. As soon as Queen Anne had stopped in front of her, she performed a perfect curtsey and kissed her new stepmother's hand.

"I am honored you have come to visit me." She met Anne's kind gaze.

"The honor is all mine. I was hoping to see all the children of my husband the King." The sentence was awkward but unsurprising given she had only been in England for a little over four months.

"I think I should introduce you to your cousins." Queen Anne looked behind her and motioned with the tilt of her head for Catherine to step forward with Kitty Howard too.

They bobbed a curtsey that was fitting for Lady Elizabeth's station as the King's illegitimate daughter.

Elizabeth seemed intrigued by the sudden growth of her family. Catherine knew that ever since her mother had died, she had been in the keeping of servants and her only family had been the King and her two siblings. Now, suddenly, she had gained cousins.

Of course, Elizabeth knew that she had relatives from her

mother's side, but she had rarely, if ever, interacted with them. Catherine knew that the last time Elizabeth had been at court was when she had been honored with carrying the baptismal cloth at her brother's baptism.

The three girls seemed to consider each other for a moment before she finally spoke.

"A picnic was prepared." The former Princess led the way.

"Will you sit beside me?" Anne was all kindness and generosity as she walked side by side with her to where the tables had been set up outside.

A small tent had been erected to protect the party from the sun.

Catherine noted card tables that had already been set up. It was already well known that the Queen enjoyed playing cards and embroidery above anything else. The Lady Elizabeth seemed intent on pleasing her.

Indeed, she recited a poem for her in both English and Latin and then presented her with a set of handkerchiefs embroidered by her own hand with the letters HA entwined with vines and flowers to represent the Queen's union for her father.

Anne, who loved children, was more than pleased with the sweet talented girl. She promised to visit her often and perhaps even have her at court for the May Day celebrations. She had not seen how the child had blanched at that, but, Catherine, who was watching her intently, noted it.

Of course, she knew that it was on May Day that her mother was arrested and thrown into the Tower. To say it had been an unpleasant day would be an understatement.

But Queen Anne of Cleves seemed sure she could wipe away all the old conceptions of the day and replace the bad memories with new ones.

Catherine had to admire her tenacity. After all, wherever

she went, the Queen was reminded of her predecessors. She wore Anne Boleyn's rubies, the Spanish jewels and lived in the rooms where Jane Seymour had labored with her child and then died. Any other woman would have been haunted by these ghosts but not her.

They returned with the tide and arrived back at Westminster in a timely manner.

The King had been in a foul mood at dinner, no doubt displeased that the Queen had dared to go to Hatfield. But she spent the evening lavishing praise on Elizabeth, saying that only a daughter of his could be so smart and well-bred. This had placated his temper somewhat.

On the day of the May Day joust, they were awoken to the sound of music playing outside the Queen's apartments.

Catherine was surprised that the King had arranged for musicians to bring in the May. Kitty Howard was leaning out the window to their rooms waving a little handkerchief at them.

King Henry was among them, disguised as a bard. But even if it wasn't for his large size, he would have stood out, for, though he carried a lute in his hands, he barely played and instead looked at the ladies who had gathered with a satisfied grin.

"He promised me he would wake me up sweetly." Kitty shared her secret with Catherine.

So this had not been for the Queen's benefit. The thought hurt her, after all she would not like it if her husband was serenading a woman under her very nose. The Queen was blissfully unaware, though, and the King had not been cruel enough to let her know the truth.

There were gifts for all the ladies of her household. From bouquets of flowers to little trinkets.

Kitty had received a string of pearls, much finer than any of the other gifts. This the Queen had noticed but said nothing for the moment. Instead, she thanked her husband for his generosity.

Catherine slipped the silver brooch hammered into the shape of the Tudor rose she received into her hat for the day's festivities.

"Who shall you give your favor to?" Henry asked Anne. From his nonchalant tone, Anne sensed a trap and was wise enough now to tread carefully.

"I was going to ask you to help me decide. I know your majesty will have chosen the best man to ride for you in the joust."

"Of course, I have a lot of experience with this. Thomas Seymour and Richard Cromwell are riding for me."

"Then I shall place my bets on them since they have been chosen by you, husband."

He smiled at that and the tension in the room dissipated. "Very well."

They paraded down to the lists as one big party. The King's men and the Queen's gentlewomen.

Catherine was unsurprised to find Francis had made his way over to her side.

"Would you grant me your favor?"

Catherine turned to face him. "You are riding?"

"Is that worry I hear in your voice?" he teased.

"Well, yes. After all, it is dangerous." She tried to look away but found his smile enchanting. A giddy feeling over-taking her.

"Then give me your favor and it shall protect me."

She saw that everyone else was distracted, so she picked

at a ribbon from her sleeve and pulled it out for him. He took the ribbon and clutched it to his heart in the chivalric fashion.

"Thank you, my lady. I hope I shall make you proud of me." He gave her a little bow, which drew people's attention, and then he ran off ahead to join those getting ready to joust.

Mistress Loew gave her a disapproving look, but Catherine merely shrugged. There was nothing wrong with giving her betrothed her favor.

They were seated in the Queen's box, and, as they had arrived, the people had cheered for Anne. She had flushed with embarrassment but waved good naturedly to them.

"Why do they cheer for her so much?" Kitty's jealousy was poignant.

"She is kind to everyone." Catherine rolled her eyes.

"She isn't pretty or anything." Clearly, Kitty had not heard her. Catherine wasn't about to indulge her jealousy and she stepped away.

Catherine studied the men in the King's box. On one side was an anxious Lord Lisle, who had returned from his post in Calais. There had been rumors of a plot, and he was here to answer the King's questions. On the other side was her uncle, the Duke of Norfolk. His head was leaned towards the King's, and the two men seemed in deep discussion. Behind them, Lord Cromwell, who was not in his usual seat of honor, kept leaning forward then leaning back. He seemed desperate to hear what the King was saying.

A blast of trumpets announced the start of the tournament and all discussion stopped as the competitors entered the ring. Catherine kept her eyes peeled for Francis but could not pick him out from the knights with their visors down. She saw the King's men immediately, for they carried his banner.

From all sides, people shouted for their favorites.

Catherine watched, not daring to blink or look away for one second as the first competitors appeared on the opposite end of the lists, their lances up and their breastplates gleaming in the sun.

It was time for the Queen to begin the match. She had a white cloth in hand and she stood by the edge of the box. With a flick of her wrist the competitors were off. The warhorses pounding the ground as they raced towards their opponents, unafraid.

All morning the men clashed. Once a man who turned out to be Thomas Culpeper was unhorsed, and the ladies had all cried out in horror as they thought he might have died. Another time, it had been her own Francis who had his helmet flung off his head. He had seemed a bit dazed but was otherwise unhurt.

Still Catherine had gasped and covered her eyes. He had seen her and had patted his breastplate over his heart, reminding her that he carried her favor and was protected.

That night, there was more dancing and frivolity. Will, the fool, juggled and danced around, making everyone laugh.

Catherine was led away into one dance after another before finally escaping and looking for Francis. She supposed she could no longer ignore that she felt drawn to him. Of course, she hadn't quite forgiven his deception, but he had not meant any harm by it. In fact, his romantic notions of wanting her to love him before knowing they were to be betrothed made him seem all the more endearing.

She found him talking to some other gentleman, but he excused himself when he saw her waiting nearby.

"Are you proud of your knight? Can you forgive me for not winning any prizes?"

Catherine grinned. "I shall but you must dance with me now to make up for it."

"That's hardly a punishment."

"It might be when I step on your toes."

Chapter Ten

With the May Day celebrations concluded, the courtiers were hungry for more entertainment. They found it not long after in the King.

He was in love again.

He didn't write poetry like he used to or compose songs, however the goldsmiths were kept busy, coming in and out of his private rooms. But it was not the Queen who was being decked out in jewels. By now his dislike of her was no secret. It was to her credit that she never complained. Her reward for this was open mockery. Catherine had come to admire Anne's strength.

The speculation over who the King's new favorite was began in earnest.

Catherine knew more than most, but she was certain it wouldn't remain secret for long. Several of the Queen's ladies would run out of the Queen's rooms to go hunting with the King, but Kitty was always first among them.

Recently, little Katherine Howard had been summoned to Lambeth by her grandmother to visit her. But this was merely a ruse to disguise the true reason as Gardiner would throw lavish parties there for the King's amusement and so she was constantly in his company.

Kitty's wardrobe was replaced with fine jewels and elaborate gowns. She seemed perfectly happy accepting these gifts and not thinking about the consequences or how she would have to repay the King's generosity.

Catherine liked to think that she didn't know what she was doing when she came running to the Queen to show her a new pearl pendant or a pair of new riding gloves. Kitty was still innocent and incredibly self-centered. The world revolved around her.

Queen Anne merely smiled and admired her new trappings.

Mistress Loew was far less accepting of Kitty's behavior. She sought to reprimand the girl whenever she could, but she didn't have the power to stop her from going when the King summoned her. Catherine was sifting through the box of thread to lay out the colors Anne requested when she overheard them arguing.

"You must send her away."

"I cannot, the King likes her company and so do I. She is a sweet girl."

"The King has likely taken her for a mistress. She puts your marriage at risk."

Catherine tilted her head to see Anne's expression. The Queen looked sullen.

"If it pleases him, it pleases me." Then she caught Catherine looking at her. "The thread Lady Carey." She held out her hands expectantly.

Catherine handed them over.

"She is your cousin."

"A distant relative," Catherine corrected, not wishing to be associated with Kitty at the moment.

"She would be mistress to the King?" Anne asked in that straightforward way of hers. No one else was around that morning to overhear them.

Yet again, Catherine was at a crossroads. It took her a moment to find her voice again as she struggled with the dilemma of being honest or lying to her. She settled on the truth for there was little Anne could do either way.

"No."

At her side, Mistress Loew frowned. "But we see how he favors her and visits her privately."

"She is an honorable and virtuous lady." Catherine had developed a habit of hinting at the truth without saying it out loud. "The King would not dishonor her so."

"What else could there be for her?"

Anne hushed her German lady and turned to Catherine. "I understand. What could I do?"

"Do whatever is necessary. Don't give him any reason to be displeased with you or accuse you of anything." The Queen had to lean forward to hear her words.

Anne looked at her, her lips pursed together in a grimace. Her features were scrunched up in a look of concern, as if to say what a cruel upbringing she must have had if she was ready with such cryptic advice. Catherine thought of the Tower and a shiver ran down her spine. She didn't want to see another Queen Anne disappear into their cold damp rooms.

It filled her with guilt to leave the Queen's rooms, but she also needed the time to clear her head. Francis had taken to making excuses to join her on her outings. However, for the sake of decorum, they were never alone.

At first, he would send her a note claiming that he was

feeling unwell and needed fresh air, asking if she would join him on a walk. Then if they went out riding, he would say it was his duty to accompany her and protect her from vagabonds lying in wait in the forest. Finally, he admitted he was beginning to miss her company.

"I am finding it harder and harder to find an excuse to be by your side."

"I think you have a good one." Catherine flashed him a coy smile as they walked through the gardens. Ahead of her Kitty was strolling arm in arm with the King.

"What is it? For if I knew then you would make my life easier."

"Well, it is obvious isn't it? We are to be married, after all."

Catherine laughed when he stumbled mid-step. The King turned round to see what had happened and scolded Francis for being so clumsy.

Taking pity on him, she took his arm and waited for him to catch his breath.

"So have I made you fall in love with me?"

Catherine scrunched up her nose. "Hardly. But you are a good prospect." She leaned in closer to him. "And I find you handsome."

He gently pinched the hand resting on his arm. "You are a cruel mistress."

Catherine grinned, she was always ready to tease him. It made her feel excited to know that she had captured his attention so fully that he was chasing after her.

These were dark days for Anne, she could see her ladies slipping away from her, but there was nothing for her to do but continue on as if nothing had happened. There was nothing she could say as the accusations began.

It started with the unraveling of a plot in Calais that would somehow have the town handed over to the French. Lord Lisle found himself locked away in the Tower along with Bishop Sampson. All supporters and admirers of the Queen.

That day, Anne Basset had the good sense to disappear from her rooms. Her mother, Lady Lisle, was locked away in her rooms, sick with dread.

Then the Duke of Norfolk finally had the revenge he was craving. On the tenth of June, Thomas Cromwell, the newly made Earl of Essex was thrown into the Tower for committing treason against his highness.

Catherine wondered if her uncle could even feel joy at his victory. He would be the King's chief advisor now. But did he not stop to think that he too could be pulled down?

She returned that evening to find Kitty ordering some servants to be careful with her trunks.

"Where are you going Kitty?"

"I am being sent back to Lambeth." But she was not pouting or sad.

"Whatever for?"

"The King wants to send me away."

Catherine gave her a look. What was that supposed to mean?

"To be safe." She smiled. "Now I must go, there is a barge waiting for me."

Catherine stepped aside to let her walk past. She didn't have to ask Kitty what she meant.

She found Francis at his post at the entrance to the King's privy chamber. He saw her pale face and called to his compatriot that he would be back in just a few moments and to excuse him if the King asked for him.

"Catherine, what is it?" He had never used her Christian name before.

"I am afraid." Indeed she was trembling and she hid her hands in the wide sleeves of her grey gown.

He nodded. "You have nothing to fear."

"I don't want anything to happen to the Queen." She leaned in to whisper in his ear.

To anyone walking by they looked like a pair of lovers sharing sweet nothings.

Francis grabbed her hands. "You cannot put yourself in danger." He paused. "Catherine, look at me."

She finally met his eyes. "Swear to me you will not do or say anything to incriminate yourself."

"What is to happen to her?"

He shook his head. "They may seek to simply annul the marriage."

Catherine bit her lip. "Katherine Howard left court today."

"Perhaps you should as well."

"Not yet, I cannot leave her alone."

"Swear to me you will not do anything, or I shall write to your mother and have you sent from here." He persisted.

"I promise." But she had to look away, knowing she was lying.

"You are my betrothed and I am honor bound to stop you from putting yourself in danger."

Catherine frowned. "You told me before that you wished me to love you."

"That is true."

"Well, how can I love a man who would turn his back on an innocent woman so easily?"

"Because it is not as simple as that, as you well know. We must look out for ourselves." He gave a heavy sigh. "Especially if there is nothing we could do. Who can stop the King? Will the Queen's brother protect her? Unlikely. Think of the northerners who rose up and were struck down with the King's pardon in their pockets." He gave her a little shake. "Come to your senses, Catherine, or I swear I will drag you away from court this very day."

"Fine. But I shall stay by her side for as long as I dare," Catherine swore.

"Think of yourself and your family first." He placed a kiss on her forehead. "That is how you survive in this cruel world."

She pushed away from him. "Would you set me aside for your own safety then?"

"Never. You will be my wife and I love you already."

"I still haven't agreed."

"You will." His confidence was endearing, but she said nothing as they both turned to hear approaching steps down the hall.

It was the Duke of Norfolk, fresh from the King's rooms.

"Ah, Lady Carey. I would have a word with you." He ignored Francis completely and Francis retreated a more respectable distance away from them.

Catherine curtseyed to him and nodded, playing the part of an obedient servant. She walked by his side as he told her what he expected from her.

"I need you to make sure the Queen doesn't send any messages."

She didn't bother arguing. "I'll do what I can, but I am just one person."

"Don't worry, I have others watching as well." He spared a moment to look at Francis behind them. "Perhaps you shall retreat from court for your wedding."

Catherine straightened, fighting the urge to protest yet

again. She would do what she liked or she would try to. She hated the feeling of being commanded, especially by her uncle.

Returning to the Queen's rooms, she found the silence eerie. The household had been cut down sharply as women had fled for one reason or another. Now, with Kitty Howard — the loudest and most flamboyant of them — gone, the emptiness was felt more.

With purpose, Catherine took a window seat with her embroidery to begin the dull work of stitching the hem of a shirt with gold thread.

Queen Anne was closeted away in her prie dieu, no doubt praying on her knees for guidance and protection. When she finally appeared with Mistress Loew at her side, she looked as though she had emerged from her sick bed. Her eyes swept over those still in her rooms, could she trust any of them?

Lady Rochford jumped to her feet sweeping her a deep curtsey. "Would you like to call for some music or play cards?"

"No, Lady Rochford." Her eyes focused on Catherine. "I think I shall sew. Perhaps you can go fetch my ambassador Karl Harst to come see me." This was a command but Lady Rochford hesitated to go. She wanted to hear what was going to be said. Catherine caught her glaring at her and smiled in return.

With a swish of her gown, she disappeared.

Anne, trying to maintain a sense of decorum, sat near Catherine, and Mistress Loew handed her the piece she was working on.

For once, it was Catherine who spoke first. She did not dare look up or speak too loudly, lest the other ladies who were sitting farther away overheard. They trusted her not to say anything, though, for she was a Howard — her loyalty would be to Kitty Howard, or it should be at least.

"You must give the King whatever he wishes." She picked up another piece of thread looking as absentminded as possible.

Anne leaned forward as if investigating the thread's color. "What does he wish for?"

"To put you aside."

This Anne had suspected and known for some time but it was quite a different thing to hear.

"But we were married before God. It would be a sin to say otherwise."

"So was Catherine of Aragon, so was the other Queen. If you aren't amicable then you will share their fates. I can say no more." Catherine saw Lady Rochford slide back into the room.

Anne nodded.

"Your grace, the ambassador is detained at the moment, he shall join you shortly."

At this Anne jumped. "What? Where he is?" There was no hiding the worry in her voice.

"The King is meeting with him."

"I see."

Catherine could have slapped Lady Rochford for her cruelty, and the malicious smile spread over her face at having caused the Queen to panic. Anne did not see it that way, though, and invited her to sit with them.

They spent a week pretending that nothing had happened. The King, claiming to be feeling ill, kept to his chambers and did not greet Queen Anne on her way to chapel as he usually did in the mornings. At dinner his place in the dining hall remained empty.

The courtiers were lapping up the dramatic turn of events. They waited like salivating dogs for their master to throw them a bone.

The first blow was struck when Catherine's Lord Chamberlain, Lord Rutland came into her rooms with an order from the King for her household to leave for Richmond.

"Why?" Perhaps this wasn't the most polite question.

"There is plague in the city and the King fears for your health."

"Is he coming too?"

"I am sure he will join you after he has concluded business here."

"Very well. I am happy to do whatever the King asks of me."

For Catherine, she knew this was just the beginning. It scared her to think that Catherine of Aragon had been sent away just like this and it had been the start of a long exile that ended with her in the grave.

Catherine was starting to lose her nerve in the silence of Richmond. Despite the grand palace they were kept in, she felt the emptiness of Richmond was choking her. They were served by a barebones court. Anne's Lord Chamberlain had stayed back, and she now only had a handful of female attendants and a gentlemen of the chamber to light the fires and carry out more menial tasks.

Still, Anne maintained the illusion nothing was wrong and that she was awaiting the King who had promised to join her soon.

Karl Harst finally made his appearance, too, and they strolled through the palace gardens. Mistress Loew walked

162

behind them to keep some distance between them and the other ladies so Catherine did not hear what was being said. But she knew it was nothing good, for the Queen could not manage a smile for him when he departed later that afternoon.

⸻

A few days later, when Catherine received a note from Francis, she could have cried from relief.

"Tell me if you'll have me and I will come take you away. – Yours, Francis"

She hesitated to reply; though her head told her to say yes and leave immediately, her heart hurt for Anne who would feel even more abandoned now. There was another letter that followed from her mother. It was the second time she had written to Catherine since she had arrived at court.

"You are to come home as soon as the Queen can spare you. I am feeling ill and need your help."

Finally, it was Lady Rochford who pushed her out the door with threats. She found her during dinner and took a seat by her side.

"Dearest niece, why do you linger here?"

"I am serving the Queen," she replied simply. Catherine straightened in her seat, trying to appear as immovable as a statue.

"Your family needs you more now."

When Catherine did not reply, she pressed onwards.

"I wonder if you are thwarting our efforts in some way," she hissed in her ear.

"I have done nothing," Catherine lied.

"You haven't slipped some advice or warning in the Queen's ear? You are so often alone together." A pause.

"Anyone might suspect something. Perhaps the two of you are plotting."

Catherine leapt around, glaring at her treacherous aunt. "I am loyal to the King. You are vile for insinuating anything. The Duke of Norfolk put me here."

"Yes, and I do believe he instructed you to leave now. Perhaps you should go before you end up creating more trouble for yourself and her. Who knows what people will report to the King or what plots can be concocted."

Catherine gulped. Her decision was made, but she didn't let Lady Rochford know that she had gotten under her skin.

That evening, she sent a messenger to Francis asking him to come fetch her home. Then she went to the Queen with her mother's message. She hoped Queen Anne would understand, but there was also little she could help her with.

"Of course, you must go to your mother. I pray that she recovers swiftly."

"I shall return to you when I can," Catherine promised, hoping against all hope that Anne would find a way to escape unharmed. She did not deserve the King's cruelty.

Francis arrived the very next day. A small retinue of Howard men and a lady in tow for propriety's sake. Their reunion was a cold one. As he cupped his hands to help her into the saddle, he tried catching her attention, but she stoutly avoided his gaze.

As they left the courtyard Francis rode up beside her.

"Lady Carey, why are you upset with me?"

"I am ashamed that I am running away. I thought I was stronger than this."

He nodded. "But it also takes strength to walk away.

Everyone will protect their own skin. That is the truth of the world we live in."

"It doesn't sound like a very honorable one."

"Perhaps not."

They traveled until nightfall, where they rested at an inn. They would have stayed at a monastery, but its doors were barred and it was empty. The King's reformation had silenced the monks inside forever.

When they arrived at Rochford Hall, Mary greeted her with an unusual amount of affection, pulling her into her arms.

"I am glad to see you have returned to me safely."

Catherine knelt for her mother's blessing. "I am happy to see you too, Lady Mother."

Her mother turned to Francis and also thanked him for seeing her safely home.

"Will you stay for dinner?"

"I shall return to my mother's house for the time being." And he turned his horse back the way they had come in.

He was out of sight before Catherine could protest.

"He'll be back. We are making preparations for your wedding."

Catherine's eyebrows scrunched up. "So soon?"

"We thought it would be prudent."

"We?"

"Your stepfather and I. He is a good match. In the King's good graces, a gentleman of a respectable fortune and a reformer."

Catherine had not known that about him. Although her family followed the King's reformed faith, they had always been staunchly Catholic. The way she prayed changed so often that Catherine did not much care for either as long as the King wouldn't say they were heretics.

"So now you will have his protection or he yours, whichever way the wind blows."

The methodical way in which her mother had chosen her husband left a bad taste in her mouth. She tried not to doubt Francis' feelings towards her. She craved to be wanted for herself, not for political expediency.

Chapter Eleven

❧❧❧

E ven as they fitted her for a wedding gown, she waited for news to come from Richmond or the court. How was Anne? Had she been entrapped into saying something that would land her in the Tower?

Finally, they heard that the divorce proceedings had gone surprisingly smooth. It had been over within three days. The former Queen, after a moment of hesitation and protest, had agreed to sign the papers put before her by the council.

It turned out she had indeed been pre-contracted, though she had sworn otherwise before her marriage. Now she was embarrassed again with the annulment of her marriage, but she was rewarded handsomely for complying so easily. She would be known as the King's Sister and was welcomed to stay in England for as long as she chose.

"The King settled a small fortune on her. Including Richmond Palace," William said, reading the letter he received from a cousin.

"She will be happy there," Catherine said, happy to know that she would not have to return to Cleves. "And the King? Has he married Kitty?"

This time her mother spoke, she had little Elizabeth in her arms. "He probably has but in secret. It's his way. You shall have to return to court to serve her."

Catherine balked at that. How could she bear it?

As if reading her mind, Mary chastised her. "You will be grateful for the position your uncle has been kind enough to give you." She had been upset that Catherine had not come home immediately when summoned and demanded her obedience now.

"Yes, Mother."

———————

Her wedding was a small family affair. She wanted nothing else. The contracts between the families were finalized and signed. Her dowry would be transferred to Francis, and her jointure was settled upon her as well.

Francis has two houses of his own and would inherit a third upon his mother's death. As a pensioner of the King's, he also received a yearly allowance from the royal treasury, so he was not a pauper by any means. Her mother explained this to her with a happy gleam in her eye.

She was happy to see her daughter so well settled, despite her dubious parentage and the stain of disgrace that remained on the family. Now with the King marrying another Howard girl, Francis's own mother was happy to overlook these impediments.

But Catherine was less concerned about wealth and status. It appeared she had inherited her mother's desire for love. He had always shown he cared for her, but she was still uncertain of how genuine it was. After all, she had seen all too often how empty words could be.

They were married from their local chapel.

Her mother and stepfather, as well as his family, were all in attendance as witnesses. Harry had been unable to attend at such short notice.

Catherine and Francis knelt before the priest in their best clothes. She fidgeted with the gold chain of the girdle around her waist which prompted Francis to squeeze her hand in reassurance.

After their vows were exchanged and the final contracts signed, the couple were led to the courtyard where her mother had arranged a picnic for the tenants and servants. They stood as each and every one of them gave their bless-ings and congratulations — occasionally, a basket of goods was handed to her.

Finally, this was followed by a feast in the great hall at Rochford. They danced well into the night, and Catherine was sure she was going to pass out from exhaustion before nightfall.

When they were put together to bed for the first time, Catherine couldn't look at him. She had become a statue, too worried to even move. She had been happy enough to joke and dance with him earlier, but, now that she was left alone with him, her fear was greater than her happiness.

He took pity on her and did nothing but kiss her brow goodnight.

"You are tired, there's no need for us to rush."

"They will say the marriage wasn't consummated." Her voice was cracking from nervousness.

"We can make sure they don't know."

"How?"

He turned her around and unplaited her hair from its braid. His gentle hands made her sigh with pleasure as he tousled her hair. Then he untied the front of her nightgown, which made her freeze, but he did nothing else but retie it in a hasty manner. Standing up, he took a needle from her chests across the room and pricked his finger, letting a few drops of blood stain the sheets.

"There," he declared, looking her over. "You look positively un-virginal."

This made her laugh but to also shift uncomfortably under the sheets.

"Good night, wife," he said after climbing into their shared bed.

"Good night, husband." With that he blew out the last remaining candle in the room.

A week later, they heard through the grapevine that the King was rumored to have married Kitty Howard. Catherine had to remind herself that she couldn't call her that any more. She would now be Queen Katherine. It sounded strange on her tongue and completely unsuited for the light girl who was too young and playful for the title of Queen.

The King had not returned to court. Instead, he continued honeymooning in the country. There was sickness in London and rumors of plague, so he began his progress around the country with his new bride by his side.

Catherine was excused from attending her until they returned to London, so she would be able to enjoy a few lazy weeks of her own with Francis. They spent two days with her family, playing with Elizabeth and riding out with Henry, who joined them on hunts around the grounds.

Henry was not as annoying as she had remembered him, or, perhaps he had matured from his bullying ways. They had plans to send him to Oxford to finish his education before joining the King's household.

Then, Francis declared that he wished to show Catherine her new home, and they prepared for the long journey to Reading. The pair left with the blessing of her parents.

They had to go around London to reach Reading from her home in Essex. Their journey would cover nearly a hundred miles. Their small retinue traveled a quick pace, but they still had to take shelter every night at an inn or great house that gave them permission. With the sickness spreading, they were met with distrust and had to bribe their way inside at times.

It was on one of these evenings that Catherine reached for her husband as they lay in bed. She brazenly took initiative and kissed him awake.

"Catherine?" He was just coming out of his sleep. "What are you doing?"

They had shared kisses and caresses in the past but now she wanted more.

"I am no longer content to just be your wife in name." He was alert at that and couldn't help but grin.

"If you are sure?"

"Quite sure." She reassured him with a laugh.

In the end, they had to spend two more days at the inn while she recovered enough to travel.

"I could have asked about a litter."

But Catherine slapped his arm. "There is no need, I am feeling much better." Indeed, the pain had gone away now after they had paid handsomely for a hot bath to be brought to her room.

By the time they finally arrived at his manor in Reading, they were clinging to each other like a lovesick couple.

"This is your new home." He announced it proudly and introduced her to the household staff assembled in the courtyard.

The two story building was of decent size, but it was the large park around it that was more impressive. Inside, the servants had scrubbed everything clean and opened the windows to let fresh air in. It was sparsely decorated but seemed to be a comfortable home.

"You shall do what you like with it," he said, knowing it did not compare to Rochford Hall.

"It's perfect for us," she reassured him.

That night as they lay side by side in the aftermath of their heated union, he turned to her.

"Mistress Knollys, tell me the truth. Are you upset by the demotion?"

Catherine sat up considering. She was no longer a lady, but she did not think it mattered too much. Not to her.

"A little, I suppose, so you shall have to find a way to make it up to me." She was grinning mischievously.

"Mistress Knollys, I am not sure this wanton behavior is proper in a wife." He pulled up the covers in mock modestly as she had leaned over to kiss him.

"Catherine," she corrected him as their lips touched.

They kept to themselves, enjoying each other and were lucky that their household avoided the sickness that now plagued London in full force.

In the mornings, Catherine would make possets from herbs, like she had seen her mother do at Rochford. Then she took over the reins of the household, making sure it was running smoothly, that their servants and tenants prayed as they were supposed to and paid their taxes and fees on time.

She took the Queen Anne's example and tried to be as generous and gentle a mistress as she had been. She didn't yell or make unnecessary demands, and they seemed to appreciate her for it. More than that, she asked for help when she did not know something, instead of imposing her own beliefs.

Francis himself kept busy hunting and going out with the steward to look at what needed to be done on the land - from making sure the flock of sheep was well tended to the wheat that was growing higher and higher in the fields. They would rely on it to feed the animals and for profit.

Their seemingly carefree days did not last long. They had been at Readings for barely two months when they received the summons to court. Catherine was to return to the Queen's side to serve as a lady in her household and Francis would return to serving the King.

"I shall have my own rooms." Catherine sighed thinking of the one happy thing about this.

"And shall you let me visit them?" He was joking, but, since they were not in private, Catherine cuffed him lightly.

They traveled to join the rest at Hampton Court without delay.

Catherine had ordered two new gowns, and she sported the stormy blue one as she entered the Queen's chambers. It did not surprise her to find the ladies in disarray. The Queen was playing with a dog, tossing the ball for it and then chasing it around the room when it refused to return it.

Other ladies were just as idle, playing on lutes or gambling.

Catherine was shocked to see how young the new ladies were. Only Lady Rochford and herself remained from Queen Anne's ladies. Lady Bridgewater, the sister to the Duke of

Norfolk, emerged from her rooms too, looking as though she was suffering from a headache.

But she did not recognize the rest of the girls.

"Oh, Catherine, you are here!" Queen Katherine said loudly when she saw her.

Catherine hesitated only for a moment before falling into a deep curtsey. "Your Majesty, thank you for having me at your court."

Queen Katherine seemed pleased with her deference. "You are most welcome. You may stand, Lady Carey."

"Mistress Knollys now." Lady Rochford stepped forward with a grin. Katherine allowed her to kiss both cheeks in greeting. "We have missed you, niece."

It didn't take long for her to notice the difference between the new Queen and the old. Katherine Howard had remained as greedy as ever, and she loved frivolity, spending much of her time dancing in her rooms rather than doing anything productive.

The King continued to shower his new bride with gifts, happy to be rewarded with her smiles and kisses. Henry seemed like a new man. Invigorated by the excitement of a pretty bride, he began riding out more frequently to hunt with her and stayed up late into the night watching her dance and perform in pageants for him. The Master of Revels was kept busy with an endless stream of requests for more costumes, more plays, more dances.

Then every night, without fail, the King visited the Queen's bed. It seemed whatever impotence he had suffered with Queen Anne had lifted. Catherine did not wish to dwell on it. After he arrived and the royal couple retreated to the Queen's bedchamber, she herself was released to go to Francis.

They would steal away together whenever they had a

moment to spare. Sometimes they would sneak off into closets or once, as the court was out hunting, they snuck off, hidden by the trees to share each other's company.

So in these early distracted days, Catherine did not notice anything amiss about the Queen except that she was as unqueenly as a girl her age might be.

The spell was broken with the arrival of Christmas and the Ladies Anne and Mary. First, the King's daughter, who arrived in the Queen's apartments, had been shocked by their appearance and the lack of decorum displayed by the ladies. Catherine had seen the awkward first meeting between the new stepmother and daughter.

At first the Queen had been gracious, but the condescending tone with which she addressed Mary insulted the former princess. Catherine had seen Mary positively glare at the Queen. She would wager the Mary was hiding a clenched fist in her long sleeves.

She was older than her new stepmother by nearly a decade. They painted a strange picture.

Unlike Anne, who had played the part carefully, Katherine Howard was unsure how to act and her attempts to play mother to Mary had been rebuffed most famously. Catherine had watched from the sidelines struggling to keep her expression impassive for the awkward meeting.

"You shall come to me if you need any new dresses. And I can assign you a chaplain and tutor," the Queen said, looking pleased with herself despite the glares she was receiving from Mary.

"Madame, you are too young to know any better, but I have been raised and prepared for my great station my whole life." Mary took a great breath. "You are merely standing in the place of greater women."

The ladies gaped at her audacity, and Queen Katherine was looking around her aghast at the way she was being treated.

But Catherine knew she had no retort.

"Y-you shall be very sorry indeed. You have spoken to me most rudely. I am your stepmother and Queen. You shall show me respect."

"If you need to ask for my respect then you have not earned it."

Katherine took a step back, clearing her throat and, like a child, threatened the infamous princess.

"I shall speak to the King. He shall be displeased you have spoken to me like this."

This finally made Mary blanch and the Queen smiled triumphantly even though running to the King made her seem more like a child than ever.

Still, Princess Mary did not ask for her forgiveness. She stood before her, waiting to be dismissed. Court protocol forbade her from leaving without permission.

At length Queen Katherine waved her away.

Then Lady Anne of Cleves arrived. The court found her much changed. Now wearing a fashionable English hood and dress, she appeared quite attractive and her gracious manners put Queen Katherine's to shame. She brought lavish gifts for the King and Queen, including a pair of matching horses trapped in purple velvet, and gave all deference to the new Queen.

The two women provided a perfect contrast to the new court growing around the Queen. They reminded the courtiers of what proper behavior should look like, and, indeed, during those Christmas days, they managed to get a hold of Katherine's ladies and make them behave.

There was no more sneaking off in the middle of the night to meet with lovers. There were no more romps late into the night. No more idle gossip and chit chat all day. They had been shamed into good behavior.

For her part, Catherine was glad to be reunited with Anne and found time to walk with her, hearing how she was settling in at Richmond. Anne never spoke of anything except pleasantries and Catherine did not dare ask more.

The Duke of Norfolk, who had arrived for the Christmas feast, had tried to rebuke his niece for her mismanagement of her household but it was to no avail. The minute Christmas was over and the Ladies Mary and Anne departed, the Queen's rooms fell into playful chaos.

Catherine did not care too much — she could have warned her uncle that this would happen. He feared that the King would find this lewd behavior unpalatable after the initial newness of his marriage wore off.

Lady Rochford and Catherine were summoned to his rooms, just like in the old days, but, unlike before, Catherine did not feel the same sort of loyalty or devotion to her new mistress.

"Has she shown any signs of being with child?"

Catherine shook her head.

"I am keeping track of her cycles," Lady Rochford offered helpfully.

"Good. It is imperative that she conceive as soon as possible. There should be no trouble, the King visits her every night."

Catherine saw Lady Rochford grimace.

"What is it?" he snapped.

"She confided in me that sometimes the King... cannot perform or struggles to do so," she whispered.

The sharp intake of breath from the Duke showed his displeasure. "She will have to do what she must. I haven't put a Howard girl on the throne again to see the chance of a Howard Prince disappear!"

"I shall encourage her," Lady Rochford was practically quaking in her shoes.

"And why can she not control her maids?" he demanded.

"She is just as silly as them," Catherine retorted, and he did not seem to like that.

"She is Queen now. The King favors her but he can just as quickly tire of her. You must make her behave."

After their lecture from the Duke, both she and Lady Rochford tried to keep things calmer in Katherine's rooms. But there was nothing to do when Queen Katherine herself instigated games.

Francis came to her one evening and asked her to come to his rooms later that night. Catherine expected he wanted her company in bed but rather he motioned her to sit by the fire.

"Do you know of a man in the Queen's rooms named Francis Dereham?"

Catherine scrunched her eyebrows thinking hard. "I have seen him. He used to live at Lambeth, working as a page for the Duchess."

Francis clicked his tongue in displeasure.

"He has been making claims that could put the Queen and your family in danger."

Now he had her full attention. "What has he been saying?"

They were speaking head to head — even if someone was listening at the door they wouldn't be able to hear anything.

"He was heard saying that he had been in the Queen's council before any other man."

Catherine bit her lip. "He could mean anything by that."

"Yes, but she often favors him and anyone could twist the meanings of his words."

Catherine gulped. "What should I do?"

"I would tell your uncle. This is too dangerous and I don't like it at all. If anything goes wrong, the King's fury would fall on you all."

As her husband suggested she went to her uncle. He seemed just as concerned but the man could be silenced.

"I'll have a man have a word with him and I'll speak to the Queen myself." He looked annoyed at having yet another disreputable girl in the family. But what did he expect? Did he not set her on her path to seduce the King into leaving his previous wife?

"Thank you for bringing this to my attention. I think I can trust you to keep your mouth shut, can't I, Catherine?"

"Yes. I don't want to be ruined by her behavior."

"We shall all be ruined if we are not careful."

The Queen's entry into London had been put off long enough, and, with some final preparations, it would finally happen in March. Queen Katherine was jumping with joy, but she was disappointed to learn that she would not be crowned.

"Why not?" She pouted and Lady Rochford, who was brushing her hair, gave it a tug to remind her to watch her tongue.

"The King will decide when. Likely after you have given

him a son. If Jane Seymour had not died, he would have crowned her."

Katherine sulked but the arrival of a pair of sable furs finer than those given to Anne of Cleves put a smile on her face again.

The royal barge was decorated with roses and wreaths hung around the boat. Katherine was dressed in a gown of silver beside her husband, who wore a stately suit made from cloth of gold. The Mayor of London, who had greeted Queen Anne just a year ago, put on yet another pageant for the new Queen.

Other barges joined the royal couple, equally decorated and filled with amusements. One had acrobats and jugglers, while another carried musicians. Everyone cheered for the pretty Queen and the guns sounded off a salute. The cannons of the ships in the harbor also greeted her with great bellows.

They feasted at Westminster and Katherine danced with her ladies all night as the King watched.

Queen Katherine was not one to forget about her family, and she was insistent upon visiting the Lady Elizabeth. On a hunting expedition with the King at Baynard Castle, she took a small entourage to meet the former Princess at Chelsea. The official excuse was to oversee the setting up of her new household.

Catherine rode at her side, intrigued by the prospect of meeting the child again. Like before, she waited prim as a rose for the party to appear, and she curtseyed neatly to the new Queen. Whatever she thought about meeting yet another Queen she kept to herself.

"You've grown so much, Lady Elizabeth," Queen Katherine exclaimed. It seemed she had taken it into her head to adopt the little girl. "I have brought you a few presents."

"Thank you, your grace."

A groom stepped forward leading a beautiful white pony with a grey mane. The pony was tacked up with fine riding gear.

Seeing she was hesitant of the horse, Catherine stepped forward. "May I help you, my lady?"

The red-headed girl nodded and Catherine wondered at the similarities between herself and Elizabeth. She lifted the girl with relative ease and showed her how to hold the reins tight.

"You look like you would make a brilliant huntress." The Queen clapped.

"I am not so good with horses," Elizabeth admitted to Catherine, but she spoke low so they wouldn't be overheard. "I am better at my studies."

"You shall improve with practice. Besides you do look handsome in the saddle. Make sure you sit up straight and don't let anyone know you are afraid."

"Even when I think I will fall off?"

"Especially not then."

The Queen had other gifts to shower on her stepdaughter who, unlike the Princess Mary, was a more appropriate age for her to fawn over and instruct. She gave her new jewels from a hood gilded with gold and pearls to a delicate chain with a diamond pendant on the end and other smaller trinkets.

Catherine noted that she should have brought the girl more books for that was what she seemed to covet most of all.

In the evening, the King surprised them all by appearing with a freshly killed buck to roast over the fire for their dinner. They spent the night together dining as a family.

It was a pretty picture of marital bliss but it could not last.

<hr />

The happy mood of the court was cut short when King Henry took to his bed at Whitehall Palace. Word spread around court that he had exerted himself in the last few months keeping up with his young wife and ignored his failing health. The doctors and physicians were sequestered in his rooms until the early hours of the morning, reviving him from the fever that had taken him so abruptly.

Queen Katherine was more than sympathetic, rushing to his side the minute he had awoken. But the stench in the room from the wound on his leg and his foul temper sent her running back out again as quickly as she had entered.

"Your grace, you should go back and beg his pardon." Lady Bridgewater was urging her to be calm.

"I will not!"

"The King is in a lot of discomfort, you would help ease his pain. You just need to be patient with him." Lady Rochford tried as well.

"He upset me and insulted me. I am the Queen and I shall not be treated like this." She rushed into her bedchamber slamming the door behind her.

The sound made everyone jump, but no one dared go in after her. No one wanted to. Kitty's temper tantrums had lost their novelty. When she emerged and was much calmer, she decided to try to go to the King's rooms again.

Catherine walked behind the haughty Queen. When they came to the King's room the Queen discovered that they were barred to her.

"What is the meaning of this?"

The men looked apprehensive in the face of her displeasure.

"The King has said he will see no one."

"Including you, your grace," the second, Thomas Culpeper, added. "I am sure he will see you once he is well."

Kitty seemed like she would protest and create more ruckus so Catherine grabbed her hand.

"Let's go to the chapel to pray for the King's health, your highness."

Kitty caught herself before entering the throes of another tantrum and agreed to go without further protest, but they did not go to the chapel. If the King was unwell then the Queen would find her entertainment elsewhere.

Indeed, she summoned musicians to her rooms and she danced the day away. Though she did not dare ride out, she found plenty of amusements in her own room.

Catherine was surprised to receive a letter from the Lady Elizabeth thanking her for her advice and letting her know that she was taking riding lessons every day. She was sure Elizabeth had also written to the Queen, but she rarely read her letters as she could barely read herself.

She found the letter touching and replied, sure that it would not hurt anyone to do so.

The next day the Queen declared she would have a dress for every day of the year and the seamstresses arrived covering her in fabrics of every color for her to choose.

With the Queen so distracted these days, Catherine too decided to do something for herself and snuck out of her rooms to meet with Francis. He was not part of the favored few given the privilege to serve the King during his illness, so he spent his time gambling, playing tennis or riding.

The sky was clear and they left Whitehall behind to wander the streets of London. They ate freshly baked bread together and a large piece of ham, then turned to the market where they investigated the stalls.

"How do you like this?" Catherine picked out a string of pearls and held it up to her neck for Francis to see.

"It is fine but not as nice as these." He held out a gold chain embossed with clusters of pearls and small oval rubies. "It will match your pretty cheeks when you blush. Ah, just so!"

Catherine covered her cheeks with her hands. "Are you playing at being a poet now?"

He shrugged and fished for his purse, paying the merchant. "I have nothing to do but think of love all day."

He turned her around so he could clasp the gold chain. "It suits you."

"It was too expensive." Though she did not complain too much.

They returned from their expedition just in time for dinner.

"Back to work with you, my sweet." He kissed her. "Keep the Queen steady."

That was getting harder and harder to do. Without the King around, the Queen was less willing to restrain her behavior.

Catherine was distracted with another secret as well. She had missed her course, and, though she couldn't be sure, she believed she was with child. It both terrified and delighted her.

At length, the King recovered first his good temper and then his health. He admitted his wife to his rooms again, and she went with a smile plastered on her face, not daring to show him that she was upset. Trained on what to say by Lady Rochford, she assured Henry that she had missed him terribly while he was ill. It had made her sick to her stomach that she had not been by his side.

As she watched her cousin recite her pretty speech, Catherine had to focus not to show any signs of amusement at this lie.

One night when Francis pulled her into bed beside him, he teased her, claiming that she was growing fat on the rich food of the court.

"It's hardly the food you have to blame for my growing belly, husband."

He was ready with a witty retort when he stopped to look at her more carefully.

"Is there something you'd like to tell me?"

"I am with child. I was not sure but it's been almost three months since I bled last."

He interrupted her with a joyous hurrah, making her laugh. "It's not as if you won at cards."

Francis splayed his hand across her widening belly. "It feels as though I have." He paused. "You shall have to go to Reading to have the baby there. The court is no place for you."

"Or in Essex with my mother."

"Whatever you want." He placed a kiss on her belly. "Anything for you."

King Henry's good mood did not extend to everyone in his realm. He brought in the spring with bloodshed.

For Catherine, who was not particularly devout, the strug-

185

gles between the Catholics and Protestants had largely gone by without her notice. She had not been at court during the great north uprisings by the Catholics nor had she witnessed the massacre that was the King's justice. All she knew was to worship God the way the King demanded. It was a sensitive subject for many people in the Kingdom, but she felt she was better off not aligning herself to one cause.

Now a fresh rebellion had been squashed and more plots to take the throne had been uncovered. There were rumors that the Catholics, with the help of the Spanish, would rise up, overthrow the King, and put his Catholic daughter Mary on the throne.

There was a scramble to burn documents, pay off servants, and hide anything incriminating as the King turned his suspicious gaze to those of the old faith. Even Bishop Gardiner thought it would be prudent to leave London for a time.

Despite the unrest, it was a shock to the court when the King had Margaret Pole, Countess of Salisbury, his kinswoman, executed on the Tower green. She had not been accused. She had not been given a trial. She was sixty-seven years old and her death was cruel. Those who witnessed her death reported that it took several blows with the axe for the deed to be done.

Even more horrifying was how close she had been to the King. Not only was she his mother's cousin, but she had watched the King play in his nursery. She had been there when his mother had died, had been there at his first wedding, and at the birth of his children. With unquestionable loyalty, she had served him and Queen Catherine of Aragon for years.

When he wanted to divorce Catherine, Margaret stood by her side until the very end. Not only for the Queen's sake but also for the sake of the King's soul. One of her sons, who was now a cardinal in Rome, took an active part in persuading the Pope not to give Henry his divorce.

It did not matter in the end. The King took what he wanted. But these acts of defiance left a bad taste in his mouth. So finally, the King who never forgot a grudge, signed her death warrant and the court was shocked into silence.

Catherine was reminded of her poor wretched aunt once more. It seemed the King's desire for blood was endless. She observed the cool detachment with which the Queen heard the news. In fact, she appeared bored at dinner by the hushed silence that came over the court and how they discussed the bad end to a good woman. It made the Queen queasy to hear of blood.

Catherine could just hear her now. What did it matter to her that an old lady was dead? After all, she was a traitor! So let's have no more of this talk and let's have some music.

Catherine put a hand over her growing belly. She no longer wanted to go on progress. For it made her sick too, realizing how easily the King could put a woman to death. There was no protection even in kinship.

She had her way. As the large court — which seemed more like a town on the move — was making its way up north, she took leave of the Queen and household to go to her mother at Rochford Hall for her lying in. Lady Rochford was positively peeved at hearing that. She was always irked by the reminder that while she had the title she had no lands to go along with it. Instead, her lands had been given over to her old rival, Mary Boleyn.

Francis saw her safely in her mother's keeping but could not stay longer than a fortnight.

"I'll try to be back before the baby is born. Stay safe." He kissed her brow and bid his mother-in-law farewell.

Such was the life of a courtier — always on the move.

He kept her abreast of the news along the progress with frequent notes and letters. Catherine was sure he would bankrupt them with all the payments to messengers. So that was how she knew all about the court's journey. The greetings and gifts — the fabulous dancing. The weather that was not cooperating, and the King's bouts of bad temper which coincided with his bowel movements.

It kept her occupied as she waited for her baby to arrive.

Her labor pains began earlier than expected. She was happy to have her mother by her side, as someone who had gone through the pain of childbirth before and came out alright. The ever-present fear of death hung over her as she pushed throughout the night. But she could not linger on her fear of death and pain — she had to focus on happier thoughts.

Finally, just after dawn, her baby girl was born.

She focused on the sound of her cries as she drifted off to sleep, utterly exhausted. There was a wet-nurse ready to feed her baby and a nurse to rock the baby and watch over her. As she kept her eyes fixated on her swaddled baby, she knew she was being tended to by the midwife and her mother who made sure she was washed and put into a clean bed. She couldn't put words to the feeling of joy welling up inside her. All she wanted to do was hold her baby, but she found she couldn't voice her desires.

She was slipping in and out of consciousness while this was happening, and, when she awoke the following day, she found her mother at her bedside with bloodshot eyes.

"I thought you had taken a fever. You had bled so much."

"I feel alright," Catherine assured her, her body felt heavy as if she was still half-asleep. "Where is Mary?"

"Who?"

"My daughter? I named her, did you not hear me?"

Her mother shook her head.

"Oh. Is she well? Can I hold her?"

"Yes, she is strong. She is sleeping right now. It's best we don't disturb her. I hope Francis won't be disappointed."

"N-no, he won't be. Mother, I'm tired now. Can I sleep?"

"Only if you promise to take some broth."

Catherine complied. The liquid soothed her dry throat, she vaguely remembered screaming until she was hoarse.

"Perhaps it's better I don't remember," she said out loud.

It took her a week to recover fully, by then her mother had sent a messenger to Francis who arrived post haste to be at her side. He marveled at the little creature they created but worried for her. He treated her more like a fragile piece of glass than a woman. He stayed for the christening and then had to return to the King's side.

"You should return as soon as you are able. The Queen needs you."

"Why?"

He looked around them in the stable yard, but there was no one that could be listening.

"There have been strange occurrences in her rooms on the progress."

Catherine raised an eyebrow. "Like what? Ghosts appearing?"

But he wasn't laughing. "Her door was locked one night."

Now she frowned too. "And I caught her making eyes at Culpeper. I am sure I am not the only one to have noticed how she favors him."

"She always had her eyes for him."

"She is the King's wife. If he should ever discover..."

"I'll join you as soon as I can."

Catherine stayed as long as she dared. It filled her with a strange sense of joy and pride to watch her daughter kick and scream.

"I don't want to go back," she complained bitterly to her mother who nodded in understanding.

"It is your duty to serve the Queen. Go and we shall look over the little one."

Catherine met up with the court at Hatfield on their way back to London.

She received much attention as she entered the Queen's rooms. Everyone inquired after her baby and what she had named it. She was more than happy to give them the details.

Chapter Twelve

It took her awhile to regain her bearings. When she did, she realized how far the Howards had come in such a short amount of time. Lord William Howard was now the English ambassador in France, Master Tilney, a Howard loyalist, was made a lord, and her uncle had been awarded new titles.

Each and every one of her relatives or family friends came for a piece of the pie.

The King, who was truly still besotted with Kitty, felt generous when it came to his wife's friends. Meanwhile, Kitty had learned how to play him like a fiddle. She knew when to be silent and what to do when his temper was flaring up. She was ready with a smile and never let him know how bad he smelled. She was taking this better than anyone could have hoped considering what a selfish girl she was.

Catherine, who had spent several months sharing a room with her, knew that something was amiss. Her cousin was altogether too happy and carefree. When she had last seen her, she was chafing against the responsibility of her new role.

She remembered how Lady Bridgewater and Lady Rochford were constantly having to remind her to keep her temper.

Her husband's warnings were at the forefront of her thoughts. Perhaps Kitty was getting pleasure elsewhere.

Catherine couldn't muse long on this as a short message came from her stepfather at Rochford. Her younger sister Anne had taken sick with a fever and died. She ran to the Queen to ask her to be excused to attend the funeral. Permission was granted and Francis escorted her home.

They spent a fortnight with her family. Harry had returned home from his studies as well, and there was a heartfelt reunion as they bid farewell to their sister.

"You must go back." Catherine shook her head at her mother.

"I can't leave you now."

"You cannot do anything else here." Her mother spoke with such cool detachment that it scared Catherine. She worried her mother would die of a broken heart.

At length, she departed with Francis. They had to plaster their fake courtier smiles once they rejoined the court. There was no room for sadness at the court of Henry Tudor this summer.

Hatfield was primed for hunting, and tents had been set up for this very purpose. One morning, as they ate their breakfast, a herd of deer grazed nearby. The King pointed this out to the French ambassador, Marillac, who seemed impressed.

With his lame leg, the King no longer galloped after them, chasing them down on horseback. Instead, his men went out for him and hunted for him or herded them towards the waiting King in his box with a crossbow ready in his hand.

With the hunting and entertainment so good at Hatfield, they stayed on a few extra days.

One evening as they were watching the men come in, Catherine spied the Queen gazing out longingly on the court-yard down below. She approached cautiously to see what she was looking at. Of course, it was not the King who was there but rather Thomas Culpeper fresh from a ride, opening up his vest to cool himself off.

"Your Grace, perhaps you should come away and sit by the fire."

"No, maybe later."

Catherine bit her lip. She saw Lady Rochford note Kitty's behavior too, but it did not shock her. In fact, she had to hide her smile by looking down at her hands in her lap. She talked to her aunt once the Queen had retired with the King.

"You do not seem concerned about her behavior," she said.

"There is nothing here for you to concern yourself about."

One of the ladies passing by heard, guessed what they were talking about and laughed aloud. "Oh Kit-I mean her grace was always very generous to gentlemen who paid her attention at Lambeth."

"What do you mean by that?" Catherine asked.

"Nothing, of course. She told us never to speak of it and I shall not." Mary Hall went away before she could question her further.

Catherine turned to Lady Rochford, who was white-faced.

"And you say you are not worried?"

"The girl is a mean gossip. She shall be sent away."

"I don't think your secrets are going to be kept secrets for long. I certainly won't stay silent." She stood but felt her aunt's tight grip on her arm.

"You shall not say anything. There is nothing to say."

Catherine struggled in her iron grip. Finally, she managed to free herself, and she saw Jane had left angry red marks on her arm. "I shall do what I think is right."

She did not sleep in her rooms that night but sought out her uncle, the Duke. He was furious to be awoken from his sleep, but, seeing her unabashed expression, he invited her to sit — something he had never done before.

"What do you know?" He poured a glass of wine for her.

Their conversation was brief. There was not much to say. The Queen was acting indiscreetly and it seemed she had a history of acting this way. Whatever gate had kept the knowledge secret for this long was opening. Whether it was by witnesses or by the Queen's own foolish actions — she would be discovered soon.

There was no way the Howards would survive this disgrace twice unscathed. But the Duke of Norfolk, with his pride, would try. He thanked Catherine and sent her back to the Queen's rooms.

"I shall not stay at court for much longer," she said as she reached for the door handle. "I will not let her drag me down with her."

"Smart girl."

By the fireplace where she had left her, Lady Rochford waited anxiously.

"Where have you been?"

"I was with my husband." Catherine lied smoothly. "Can you not sleep?"

Jane did not bother answering but glared at her suspiciously. With a fake yawn Catherine declared she was tired herself and went to her own room.

Catherine did nothing other than warn her husband. He was unlikely to be caught up in all of this and did not fear. But he knew that whenever the Queen was put on trial her ladies would be as well.

"I want you to make an excuse and leave court before we arrive back at Hampton Court."

"I'll say I have to move Mary to Readings."

Francis nodded. "And stay there until I tell you to come back. Don't listen to anyone else."

"I'll let the Queen know tomorrow."

They enjoyed a last night together, knowing they would be separated yet again.

Queen Katherine was in a jovial mood and could barely hear what Catherine was saying.

"May I be excused, your grace?"

"For what?"

"A few weeks to settle my daughter in her new home."

"Oh! Of course, but you will miss a wonderful celebration on All Saints Day. Are you sure you want to miss it?"

"I will see it next year."

"Very well." The Queen kissed both her cheeks in farewell and Catherine curtseyed to her.

She was in the stable yard with a hired escort of two men before Lady Rochford even knew she was gone. In any case, what could she say to stop her?

Her mother was surprised by her sudden reappearance, but Catherine refused to explain further except that the court was yet again unsafe.

In a week, her fear was justified as Francis sent her a written message by a trusted servant that the Queen was under investigation. There had been no warning except that one night the King had simply disappeared from Hampton Court.

Among her judges were Admiral Fitzwilliam who had now taken over the position of Lord Privy Seal, Sir Anthony Browne and Baron Russell. These men had served at one time or another under Cromwell and were notable Protestants.

Even Catherine knew the real prize for them was taking down the Howard faction at court with their dangerous Catholic agenda. It was an endless cycle of courtiers trying to topple each other. For now, they had caught Katherine Howard in their web, and when they discovered that Francis Dereham had been her lover while she was at Lambeth, they did not spare the King's feelings and told him everything.

Surprisingly, Henry, the cold-hearted monster, had broken down in a fit of anger and despair. In the end, he had her imprisoned at Syon House for further questioning. The Duke of Norfolk was questioned, and the Duchess, in whose household she had been raised, was as well.

It was only a matter of time before the axe found its mark.

Catherine, sick with worry that the King's men would be riding up the road to take her in for questioning, suffered through sleepless nights. She had no appetite and was often sick in the mornings.

"You must eat. They will not come for you now. You are hidden by your husband's name just as I am hidden by the Stafford name."

As time dragged on Catherine did manage to sleep more, but her appetite showed no signs of returning. She distracted herself with watching over her daughter who had seemed to double in size since the last time she had seen her.

For Christmas, Francis returned to them and was shocked to see Catherine looking so sickly.

"Dearest, you must take care of yourself."

She promised she was trying to. "I just can't seem to eat anything. It makes me sick to my stomach."

"Perhaps we should call a doctor."

"Tomorrow. Now tell me what happened?"

"I won't go into details. But Henry Manox was taken to the Tower and questioned. Francis Dereham is accused alongside him for improper behavior with the Queen."

"But she wasn't married then."

"Yes, but Francis was given a place in her household, and they suspect there may be more to the story."

"They have enough to annul the marriage."

Francis nodded and looked away.

"But that's not enough for them?" It came out sounding like a question but Catherine was truly horrified at the thought. It was an all-out witch-hunt.

"They are questioning Lady Rochford too. Your uncle, though, has escaped the King's wrath."

Catherine always assumed he would. He was a survivor and that made him dangerous.

"What are they questioning Lady Rochford about?"

Francis shrugged. "I don't know but perhaps she was witness to the Queen's behavior. If she was, then it's treasonous she didn't report it."

"I didn't report it either." Catherine gulped.

"You told your uncle, that is enough. Besides, you are safe here. Hush."

After they celebrated the New Year, Catherine was still not quite recovered and they called in a doctor who listened to her symptoms, and then, after asking her a few questions of his own, gave his diagnosis.

"Mistress Knollys, I think you are with child."

"What?" Her mouth was gaping like a fish.

"A midwife can confirm it. This is not my area of expertise." He packed up his tool bag and left the room, quite embarrassed himself.

Catherine looked at Francis who was laughing.

"Sweet wife, this explains everything does it not?"

Catherine blushed. She had thought she was so afraid she had made herself sick with worry.

"My goodness at this rate we shall have a brood of children."

Catherine looked aghast. "I would be happy with just a few."

Francis chided her. "Whatever God blesses us with will be absolutely perfect."

It was indeed confirmed that she was with child, and, as January drew to a close, Catherine believed that her cousin who was still imprisoned at Syon might eventually be freed. The King couldn't possibly bring himself to kill a young woman over a previous indiscretion.

Unfortunately, in February, they heard from London that Culpeper was arrested, and he confessed to liaisons with the Queen. The minute Catherine heard this, she knew her cousin was a dead woman.

There was no way Henry would forgive her making a cuckold out of him.

Poor Kitty went from Syon House to the Tower and only came out again to put her head down on the scaffold. Lady Rochford followed soon after. The cruel woman, who had blatantly betrayed yet another of her mistresses to save her own skin, suffered the same fate.

Francis had to return to his work at court, but, seeing as there was no longer a Queen to serve, the ladies had been temporarily disbanded. Catherine decided to put her own household to rights. She prepared for Mary and her nurse-maids to travel with her to Reading where she planned to rebuild a nursery for her children.

Along the way, she stopped by Richmond Palace and paid a visit to Lady Anne of Cleves who welcomed her as warmly as ever.

"What a pretty daughter you have." She complimented the sleeping child.

"Just wait until you hear her scream. I don't know how it will be with two babies in the house." Catherine patted her ever expanding belly.

Anne chuckled. "It's a blessing."

"Yes," Catherine agreed, realizing for the first time that Anne would likely never be a mother herself. She could never marry while the King or the Duke of Lorraine lived, since her own marriage had been annulled due to the pre-contract. Even then, if she remarried, she would forfeit the lands given to her by the King. She would be left penniless. No man of good breeding would want her.

"Do you still remember your German?" Mistress Loew appeared.

"Ja, but very little. We shall have to practice."

Anne, who was in a constant battle with her accent, laughed. "You sound funny when you speak German, just as I do when I speak English."

They talked of other affairs, but, in the end, the conversation circled back to Kitty Howard.

"She was a sweet girl." Anne remained steadfast in her opinions. "Meant no harm."

"Bah!" Mistress Loew was much more critical. "Sinful girl. It's a shame to think she seduced the King away."

"She has been punished now." Catherine stopped her before saying anything treasonous.

"True."

Then they were silent wondering for a moment who would be next? Who would dare to stand by Henry's side as his wife?

Chapter Thirteen

R eading had changed in the four years since she had taken up residence. She had the walls inside painted with white stucco, new tapestries were brought in and furniture as well. Soon they would need a bigger house, for they already had five children in the nursery. One for each year of their marriage.

Catherine's younger brother Henry Carey had wed Anne Morgan the year before, and they were living at Rochford Hall. He would run for a seat in Parliament and make his way through the world that way.

Between the blessings and the good times, there had also been sorrow.

Her mother had passed away three years ago and her younger sister Elizabeth a few months after of the sweating sickness. Her stepfather had left to serve in Scotland, and she wasn't sure if she would ever see him again.

It felt as though their family had become fragmented.

"Come to court with me," Francis said.

"Once Edward is weaned."

"Catherine, if it's Edward now, next year it will be another babe. It seems you will always have that excuse."

"I went to court to see you off to war when you sailed for France," she said.

"That was two years ago."

"And I suffered enough that time." Indeed, the court had been rife with conflict, and she had been worried for Francis' safety. The siege of Boulogne had lasted four months, but she had not known if he was safe or not. It was heralded as a great victory for the English, but the King had not reached Paris as he had hoped.

The Spanish Emperor Charles had failed to do his part and their whole campaign had fizzled down to nothing. It had also bankrupted the crown in the process. Catherine still felt the effects of the taxes the King had levied to pay for the expedition. They had managed to stay out of debt, but there was very little money left and she had taken to penny pinching.

Francis gave her a look but she knew she had won. It was hard for him to get her to leave their children and newly renovated home.

The court had become a very different place under the influence of the new Queen, yet another Catherine. It was now a center of learning and religious debate within the Kingdom. She had lectures in her rooms and had no fear in arguing with the great men of the realm over theology. The Queen was even working on a book of translations, and, though she did not put her own name to it, everyone knew her as the author.

It was a great gamble to take a position so openly, especially in King Henry's court. Where factions fought to pull each other down.

Catherine, who had been taught to speak three languages,

had not been taught to debate with men. So she felt out of place when she had stayed at court, though she enjoyed being reunited with her cousin the Lady Elizabeth who, thanks to Catherine Parr, had been reinstated to the succession.

Lady Elizabeth had grown more beautiful each year. There was no mistaking her sharp wit and intelligence. They kept regular correspondence with each other. Catherine would write to her of family news and practice her French while Lady Elizabeth would keep her abreast of court gossip. At least the gossip that was safe to write about.

It was clear that under Catherine Parr's tutelage, Elizabeth had become a firm supporter of Protestantism.

Catherine's own husband believed in the cause wholeheartedly, but Catherine was too cautious to say anything one way or another. She believed in God, did she believe that the wine turned into blood during the mass? She couldn't say.

She hid behind the ignorance of being a woman, and, though Francis encouraged her to read books he brought her, she dared not touch them in fear of one day being called a heretic.

The pyres at Smithfield were waiting for any accused of heresy, and, in this day and age, the King decided what that was. Most dangerously, his opinion from the morning changed in the evening, so Catherine took the safe route of silence.

On a sunny day in winter, she decided to have a little feast for the children in the dining hall. Since her youngest children were still toddling around, she had the tables moved away and arranged carpets and cushions in the middle of the floor like a makeshift picnic. They were sprawled before the fire, enjoying little treats from the kitchen. Her eldest, Mary, was now steady on her feet and ran around chasing after a puppy and pulling at her younger brother's hair. Only Henry, who was four years old, could chase after her to get his revenge.

As she called after the pair to not stray too far, she noticed the dust being kicked up on the road from the window. She narrowed her eyes to get a better look. It was a rider coming up quickly to the house. She stood and told the nursemaid to watch over the children and keep them safe.

By the time she reached the courtyard, the messenger was talking to her steward.

"Mistress Carey! You have an urgent message from your husband." He ran over to her with a sealed letter.

Catherine tore it off, fearing the worst, that he had taken some illness in the city.

"There is good news and bad. Rest assured I am in perfect health as I hope you and the children are as well. I am to be knighted by the King as part of a New Year's celebration. But your Uncle the Duke of Norfolk and his eldest son have been arrested. You are to come to court and be questioned. Have no fear of your safety but come as soon as you can. Be careful on the road and kiss our children for me. Love Francis"

Her hands trembled at the thought of being questioned. What was there for her to tell?

Still, she obeyed the summons. She spent the mornings with the Queen in her rooms, though she did not have an official position, and the evenings in Francis' arms. She was happy to be among women for a change and make idle chit chat with them. Other times, she would play a game of chess with Lady Elizabeth.

But whenever conversations turned to something more serious, Catherine would smile and make some excuse to go away. She was then called in before a panel of lords and ordered to sit in judgement. Edward Seymour in the center of them all.

"Mistress Knollys, you are here to answer our questions to the best of your knowledge. Do you understand?"

"Yes." She fought the urge to fiddle with the ring on her finger.

"If we find you have lied or hidden anything away, you shall face the full wrath of the King."

Catherine nodded. She did not plan to defend her uncle. He had taught her to look out for herself and leave a drowning man behind to save your own skin. He likely had never thought he would be the one left to suffer alone, but there was nothing for it now.

"Has the Duke of Norfolk ever spoken about his desire to covet the throne?"

Catherine's initial response was to say no. After all, he had never said it outright. "My Lords, I never heard him say he wanted the throne himself." She saw them frown with irritation but she quickly went on. "When the King was married to his niece Catherine Howard, he would always say how he hoped a Howard Prince would one day sit on the throne."

This intrigued them. Of course, the words would probably be twisted, but they had also been dangerous. He should have said Tudor Prince.

"He thought of himself as overly great?"

Catherine could have laughed if she wasn't nervous to be sitting before their scrutiny. "He always thought of himself as a powerful Lord of the realm. If he plotted anything more I was not aware. He didn't think much of me except as a poor relation, and I have not spoken to him since I left the service of my cousin."

"And during your time at court? What did he have you do?"

Spy. Lie. Catherine bit her tongue. "I reported to him what happened in the Queen's rooms. Such as if she was in good health or who she had seen. But he mostly turned to Lady Rochford for information or plotting."

They had a few other questions too, but she had not been witness to the events they asked her about. The men made their notes and nodded.

"Very well, Mistress Knollys, that is all for now."

Francis waited outside the chamber for her to emerge.

"You look a bit pale," he said anxiously.

"It's not every day I am questioned."

By the end of the week, Catherine had a better grasp on understanding just what her uncle had done. His eldest son had taken the arms of Edward the Confessor as part of his personal heraldry. This was to bring attention to their royal lineage, something that Henry Tudor would not tolerate.

As it turned out, she was among many who gave evidence against her uncle. Even his wife, daughter and mistress had been quick to volunteer evidence. It came as no surprise when he was moved to the Tower and sentenced to death.

His son, who was arguably more guilty, was beheaded a day after the sentencing, but her uncle, who pleaded and gave his lands and titles freely to the King in exchange for his life, was temporarily spared.

"Why do I get the feeling he will escape?" Catherine shivered as they rode away from London. If he ever escaped he would know her for an enemy now.

Riding beside her, Francis was skeptical. "I don't think he will. The King signed his death sentence."

She should have placed a bet with Francis for she would have won.

Before the sentence could be carried out, her true father King Henry Tudor died and the previous Duke of Norfolk continued to languish in the Tower.

There was more rejoicing at the King's death than sorrow.

In his later years, he had become a tyrant to his people. His rule had failed to be the Golden Age he had promised in his youth.

Now they were celebrating the coronation of his young son Edward and the end of Henry and his spies.

"These will be uneasy times," Francis predicted. "King Edward is too young to rule on his own and the council will fight over who will control him."

"We shall stay away from it all, won't we?"

"Until it is safe. The only way forward for our family is through the court. We need the fees and to make new allies. One day our children will have to marry, and I don't want them to marry into the families of our tenants."

"I did not think you had such ambitions for them."

"I know you have them as well." He gave her one of his brilliant smiles. "The world is changing. It won't be like it was before, where the King is ready to execute innocent men and women on a whim."

Francis had been right for a time. But corruption was rampant in the court as the council took advantage of the King's young age to snatch up fees and taxes without paying them into the royal treasury. The King was on the constant brink of bankruptcy. Anne of Cleves, who was still living at Richmond, was no longer paid her yearly allowance and she had been instructed to vacate the palace. They moved her to a more frugal residence — Penshurst Place, where the exchequer paid her living costs but she had little money of her own now.

She wrote dryly to Catherine that she was reduced to bargaining in the markets for cheaper prices and had taken to eating fish more often. She assured her that this was not from religious fervor but rather from practicality.

Catherine could do little to help her old mistress. Her husband, who was now widely known as a Protestant, had been given a place in the privy chamber but he was never paid his due. The exchequer simply forgot, he explained to her.

There was no reason to complain. At least he could collect bribes and fees from people to make introductions. So she too was reduced to living off their lands. Despite her endless stream of pregnancies, she traveled between Reading and the lands they held in Oxfordshire to make sure they were reaping all they could from the land.

They still had it better than some.

The Prince, who had been raised so strictly in the Protestant faith, sought to impose it on his people. There were frequent uprisings, especially in the summer after a crop failure or when he had tried to institute a bible written in English. They had been thankfully put down, but the unrest in the country was only growing.

While Francis rode out to fight for the King, Catherine remained at home trying to keep their servants and tenants loyal. She made no secret that she would report any disloyalty and would not tolerate it in her home.

In her secret heart, she prayed for better times. Her children were growing up in tattered clothing that she could not afford to replace, and they were without the proper education they should have been receiving. Catherine told herself it was better to be frugal now and get them clothes when they would go to court or were fully grown, but it hurt her to think they were failing to provide for them.

In the summer of 1553 rumors began circulating that the King had fallen seriously ill. Catherine paid them no attention until her husband confirmed it. She prayed for his recovery as she thought of a bleak future with the Catholic Princess Mary on the throne. Mary was likely to try to undo all the changes her brother had brought to the country, and that would only mean more fighting.

Catherine wasn't the only one to think this. Secretly, the councilors worked to persuade the King to change his father's will. In an effort to make sure Princess Mary would not inherit, they disinherited her and the Lady Elizabeth in favor of Jane Grey.

On the death of the King, just six years after he had come to his throne, the Lady Jane Grey was proclaimed Queen.

The people of England felt cheated and would not stand for what they had seen as injustice. It was not a matter of religion to them. Princess Mary, who at first was chased after by Dudley's army, was now doing the pursuing. She was sure to march in London and take her rightful place as Queen any day now.

Francis rode out with his tenants in support of the Princess as well. He was doing his duty to the country, but he was also not welcomed by the Catholics. Catherine begged Francis to return home, and, when he finally complied after Mary's coronation, he arrived home like a defeated man.

"I have a letter from your cousin, Lady Elizabeth." He pressed the letter in her hands.

"What does it say?"

"She asks if we shall remain loyal to her come what may."

Catherine did not hesitate. "Of course. But what is going to happen?"

"Queen Mary has come to her throne, but Elizabeth is worried that their differences in religion will cause problems."

Catherine's eyebrows rose in surprise. "They would fight over religion?"

"She has spoken to me in confidence that she will never relinquish her faith, but her sister might disinherit her or worse."

Catherine crossed herself. "Mary Tudor wouldn't dare." She remembered her as a sweet tempered woman who was generous and kind.

"She has become hardhearted."

"Can she just not pretend to convert?"

Francis gave her a piercing look and she looked away. He disapproved of her light take on religion, but she could not help herself.

They moved from Oxfordshire back to Reading to be closer to London and stay abreast of the news from the city.

Mary and her army's arrival had led to much acclaim and celebration in the city. The citizens of London were cheering in the streets as her makeshift court of loyalists followed behind her.

Lady Jane Grey was imprisoned in the Tower to await Mary's judgement and plans for a grand coronation were underway.

Francis told her how the Lady Elizabeth had ridden out to greet her sister and was present alongside the Lady Anne of Cleves at her half-sister's coronation. The people of London had also cheered for the Queen's pretty younger sister. This did not win her any friends among Mary's courtiers. Some of the Catholics commented wily that she had waited until the last possible moment to declare her friendship.

The Queen was beginning to roll back the clock on the changes made by her brother and even her father, though there was no formal declaration of a return to Rome. There was no official change to the law, but images of Saints reappeared in churches, mass was conducted in Latin.

Gold chalices and vestments were once again placed at chapel altars as slowly Catholic exiles began returning to their country of birth, happy to see the old faith returning.

Francis fretted as these changes were being made.

He would not be welcomed at court now, and he worried that the Queen would begin persecuting those she saw as heretics such as himself.

When talks began of a marriage between Queen Mary and Prince Phillip of Spain, Catherine noticed her husband sequester himself away in his records rooms. He sent out letters every day, but, when she asked him, he would kiss her and tell her not to trouble herself.

She was with child again. Her tenth. She was no longer young, but she was well practiced at this. So far, she had been blessed and her family proved to be fertile. Her children were her one source of stability and joy in this world of constant upheaval.

Her brother had a growing brood of his own at Rochford. It puzzled her to think how the Tudors had struggled to produce children and especially heirs when it seemed to come so easily to her family.

"We should go visit your brother at Rochford."

It was the start of summer, sickness was spreading and her belly had grown round. It was hardly the time to go traveling around the countryside. Her husband knew this, how could he suggest it?

"That is ridiculous! We cannot."

The way he couldn't meet her eyes made her instantly suspect something.

"I sold this house," he walked away from her as if to distance himself from her rage.

She was stunned. "What? You can't be serious! Our finances aren't so bad. And our house in Oxfordshire?"

"Gone. The sale was finalized last week." Francis ran his hand through his hair. Strands of silver glinted in the sunlight.

"Explain yourself immediately, or I swear I shall never speak to you again." There was a pain in her chest. In their many years together, he had kept his promise and never lied to her. Now she discovered he had uprooted their life.

"Catherine, I didn't want you to be distressed." ·

She gave him a scathing look and tried to calm herself as the baby in her belly grew more agitated. He looked concerned and set out a chair for her. She pushed his arm away when he offered to help.

"I kept some news from you, but only until I could discover more and figure out a plan."

"I could have helped you figure out a plan." She shot back at him.

"Hugh Latimer has been imprisoned and more shall follow. A friend at court warned me that at her first parliament Queen Mary will restore the six articles of faith. She is also intent on the Spanish marriage, and her husband will surely bring the inquisition upon our heads."

Catherine's eyebrows furrowed in confusion and a hand went to her stomach. "We will comply with the changes! Surely we cannot be accused of anything if we follow the law. You still haven't told me why you had to sell the houses."

Francis came forward and knelt at her feet, taking her hands in his.

"Wife, do you not know what the inquisition is like? I have been known as a supporter of reform for nearly all my life. Our neighbors will be quick to report me when it comes down to it. It won't matter that I have recanted. There will be questions — and they shall not be afraid to use torture to get what they want. They shall purge this country of all true believers."

Catherine shook her head, refusing to believe. Had they not survived through the last chaotic years of King Henry's reign? Had they not pinched and saved their way through King Edward's reign?

"They will not stop with me. They will come after you and the children. I hear reports of such dreadful tales from Spain. There is another thing. She has freed your uncle the Duke of Norfolk and returned him to his lands and titles. He will not forget that we gave evidence against him."

"You cannot know that this will happen. Mary was always so kind." Catherine lost her conviction.

"It's already begun. I am not a blind man to ignore the signs. Just like the Catholics fled England years ago, so must we now."

This caught her attention. "You are planning for us to leave? Where would we go?"

"Germany." He was rewarded with a gasp of surprise. "The money from the sale of our lands will see us through."

"We cannot go so far!"

"Your old mistress, the Lady Anne of Cleves did." He gave her a reassuring squeeze of the hand. "It is a Protestant nation and the only place we can be safe. I have been writing to my connections there and to others here in England. We shall not be going alone, but go we must."

"When?"

"Within the year, before the marriage takes place. They might close down the ports and prohibit travel. Don't speak to anyone about this. Let the servants know we have been having money troubles and have had to sell. "

Catherine stopped him.

"No, what if the marriage doesn't take place at all? I've heard gossip as well. Her councilors are against the match and the lay people don't want to see a Spanish consort on the throne of England. We've been at war with the Spanish off and on my whole life." She took her hands out of his grip. "Besides, this baby will be too weak to travel. You must promise me we will wait. I will agree to go but not this year. Not until we are absolutely certain of the danger."

They regarded each other for several moments — Catherine daring him to object. He stood and she knew she had won.

"Your brother has said he could house us in the meantime."

"It will take a while to pack away the house or did you sell our furniture too?"

"I have not but we can only take so much. I shall let you decide."

"You are too kind," she said sarcastically.

They had an awkward week in which she could barely look at him without displeasure showing on her face. Word that they had sold their houses got around, and the servants were all worried about their jobs. They could barely contain their own bitterness towards them.

The new owner might choose to employ other servants and they'd be out on the streets.

Catherine blamed this on Francis who staunchly ignored the complaints.

They would only keep the three nursemaids employed to help with the children. They were too young to be without constant supervision. Francis complained about the cost, but Catherine raised an eyebrow at him.

She hadn't made these children on her own.

Chapter Fourteen

By September, they had moved to Rochford. Their children thought this was a fun adventure; only their three eldest Mary, William and Lettice noticed something amiss with their parents. They were used to traveling between houses but never with great wagon loads of stuff to follow after them. They hadn't seen their beds dismantled and packed away before.

"Mother, when are we going home?" Lettice, who was the most outspoken finally, asked. Her elder siblings were hiding behind the door.

"This shall be our home for now." Catherine couldn't lie to them but nor could she trust her children with the truth.

"Are we poor relations now?"

Catherine frowned. "Where did you hear that?"

"George..." That was her brother's son.

"Well he doesn't know what he is talking about. Don't let him say such things. We are here temporarily and because my brother was kind enough to let us stay with him. Don't forget you are the daughter of a well-respected knight."

"But he hasn't been invited to court."

"Lettice, go play with your siblings. This is not something you need to worry about. Either of you." She called out this last part.

"I would like to go to court." Lettice managed to say this but in a whisper, as if she was admitting her greatest desire.

Catherine felt like a hand was clenching around her heart. She too had dreamed of life at court.

"I am sure one day you will attend court and be the most beautiful lady." She patted her fair cheeks. Indeed, she was the prettiest of all her daughters and the one who resembled her Tudor heritage the most with blazing red-copper hair to match the Lady Elizabeth's.

"And me too?" Mary popped her head in through the doorway.

"I am sure all my children will serve at court."

Later that month, as her husband had predicted, the Queen restored the church doctrine to the six articles of faith set down by her father, though there were rumors she wanted to do more than this. The nobles who had purchased church lands all feared that it would be taken from them, and the mood in the Kingdom was apprehensive even as the Catholics rejoiced.

With Rochford so crowded by children, Catherine had her hands full just overseeing their tutors and the nursemaids caring for them. She had given birth to a daughter who had been baptized Anne.

She stayed out of her brother's wife's way. Lady Anne Morgan had a fiery disposition and hated to feel that she wasn't master of her own domain. If it had been up to her, she would have surely refused to house them, but Catherine's brother had proved to be more than generous. He was the only one in the household that knew of their plans to go into exile.

So many months had passed that Catherine was certain Francis would see the error of his ways. Cranmer had been imprisoned and executed too, but this was hardly the beginning of an inquisition.

Thomas Wyatt had led a foolhardy rebellion against Mary to put Elizabeth on the throne in her stead. His reason had been the unpopular Spanish marriage, but he had failed and Catherine spent many nights worrying for her cousin who was being questioned about her involvement.

Lady Elizabeth had grown too smart to be caught up in a plot. Much to Mary's dissatisfaction, no concrete evidence could be discovered and she was set free from the Tower, though she remained under house arrest.

So Catherine was sure that all would be well.

But then one night, as her husband slipped into her bed, he pulled her into his arms and held her for a long time, stroking her hair.

"Dearest, I found a ship to take us to Germany. It is time, the Spanish are coming and a cardinal from Rome following in their tracks."

Catherine felt hot tears pouring down her face. "Not yet. Not yet."

"At the end of spring. Anne is nearly a year old. She will be fine."

It wasn't only worry for her youngest child that made Catherine hesitate though. All she had ever known was here in England — she didn't want to leave. But in the end, they did flee like criminals from their own country in the middle of the night. Though they were hardly stealthy with their ten children in tow and the crying protests. Her children had not learned fear and to be silent. In a way, they had been blessed.

As their hired ship set sail with other fleeing exiles, the Spanish boats were pulling into the harbor.

Catherine kept her eyes focused on the English coastline, wishing to imprint it in her memory forever. She clutched a note in her hand from her cousin Lady Elizabeth wishing her a safe journey and one day a safe return. She knew that it would not be possible unless Elizabeth survived to inherit her father's crown.

The culmination of all Howard ambitions would be achieved then.

The thought of a girl achieving them made Catherine smile. It seemed to have been the women of her family that had made the family's fortunes. She would pray every night for her return to England — she would see Elizabeth crowned.

The seas had been surprisingly calm, and they settled down in Frankfurt in December.

First they rented a small townhome in the merchant quarters of the city. They enjoyed their English neighbors, as they found communicating with their German counterparts hard. Catherine had forgotten a lot of the German she had learned and she sat with Francis as he learned with a tutor.

It was unclear how long they would be here. It was important they assimilate.

Her children now had a German nursemaid as well as an English one, and it made her cry when little Anne's first words were in German not English. She couldn't help but think they were losing themselves in this new country.

Once Francis' German improved, he found work as a translator, as they could not survive on the income from the sale of their houses forever.

They rarely talked of England. The news from London was bleak. The Queen, in an effort to stamp out heresy in her Kingdom, was burning heretics with a vengeance. Even her father had not been so zealous.

It had become a secret they kept from their children whenever the older children asked when they were going home. The response was always the same: one day soon.

Then Francis was invited to join other English exiles in Strasburg. John Jewel and Peter Martyr were influential men in the region and keen to gather more supporters around them.

Catherine was not surprised that they were to move yet again.

"I promise we shall have an even bigger house."

But she shifted away from him. "And what will they have you do?"

"I shall help them research and publish manuscripts on theology."

Catherine frowned. "You are hardly a scholar. Please, don't tell me you wish to become a priest now."

"No, but I would like to have Godly work to do. They are being more than generous to take me on as a secretary." Seeing she was unconvinced, he added, "And they receive frequent news from England. We shall be kept up to date."

She sighed, exasperated. "I shall follow you wherever you go but don't expect me to be happy about it."

He kissed her brow. "Sweetheart, you don't know how grateful I am that you are my wife. I promise I will make it up to you. One day soon we shall settle down again in a home of our own."

"And you won't leave me?"

"I will try not to." At her frown, he kissed her again, this time on the lips. "What if I promised you to retire early and spend endless days in the country with you?"

"I can live with that."

So it was in Strasburg that they heard the Queen was pregnant yet again. The last child had failed to materialize, but she must have been certain this time to announce it so publicly.

Catherine was surprised when Francis told her he had hired another tutor for their children and that she should order more clothing made in the latest fashions for the whole family.

"Can we afford the expense?"

"They need to have a proper education." His eyes alight with pleasure. Catherine knew he was up to something.

"What is it?"

"I don't think it will be long now before we are recalled to England." It had been nearly four years since they had left. Catherine had started losing hope.

"But the Queen might have a child now, and then Elizabeth will never take the throne."

Francis shook his head. "I have it on good authority from Master Jewel that the Queen is not with child but is ill. There won't be long to wait now."

"That could just be speculation."

"Shall we place a wager on it?"

"Five pounds."

"Done," he shook her hand with a grin.

"Robert, apologize to your sister this instant." Catherine had Robert by his ear. "And where has Edward run off to?"

Lizzy was crying at her side.

"I'm sorry I stole your doll." He muttered under his breath and squeaked when Catherine gripped him harder. "I'm really sorry, please don't cry."

Catherine released him. Lizzy rubbed her eyes and nodded.

"If you don't learn to behave yourself, I'll have your father lock you in the brig without your supper. Now where is Edward?"

"He said he wanted to go see if the Captain would let him steer the ship."

Catherine clicked her tongue with displeasure. "Take Lizzy to Mary. I swear the Captain will have us thrown overboard, we are causing him so many problems."

She marched over towards the quarter deck only to find Edward being led away by Francis.

"Go to your room." She saw him urging him away. He scampered off, happy to oblige in order to escape her wrath.

"Our children are hooligans." He took her arm and led her to the prow of the ship.

"You must forgive them. They've been cooped up on board for several days."

They watched the water lap at the side of the boat as it carried them forward. They took comfort in each other's company.

Catherine's eyes were fixed on the horizon, so she was one of the first to spy the first hint of land.

"Land Ho!" Someone shouted and there was a cheer from the sailors on deck.

"I never thought this day would come."

He gave her shoulders a squeeze, and she felt her husband brush a tender hand over her yet again growing belly.

She thought of the new challenges and political turmoil awaiting them, but they were home. Come what may, they would serve their country and new Queen Elizabeth.

"For England and St. George, onward!" She repeated the old battle cry.

Afterword

Catherine Knollys would go on to serve as a lady at the court of her cousin Queen Elizabeth I for many years. Though never acknowledged as a half-sister, she was favored by the Queen and her husband was rewarded with titles and lands. Thirteen of her fourteen children with Francis survived infancy. Unfortunately, she died at the relatively young age of forty-five; Francis never remarried.

As Anne Boleyn's niece, she lived what must have been a tumultuous life, witnessing the reigns of nearly all the Tudor monarchs.

Her brother Henry/Harry Carey had sixteen children with Anne Morgan. He served as a Member of Parliament and was eventually created Baron Hunsdon by his cousin Queen Elizabeth I. The Queen would also rely on him as a Captain-General, and he led the army in her defense several times. Henry also served as Lord Chamberlain of the Household. He died at the ripe old age of seventy.

Lettice Knollys was perhaps the most famous of Catherine's daughters. She grew to have a striking resemblance to Queen Elizabeth. She was first married to Walter Devereux,

Viscount Hereford, but their marriage was tempestuous and she was even accused of hastening his death (she was having an affair). Then in secret, she married the Queen's favorite, Robert Dudley, causing the Queen, out of jealousy, to banish her from court. At one time, it was thought that Robert Dudley might marry the Queen herself.

Made in the USA
Middletown, DE
17 August 2021